D0169879

ALSO BY GENE WILDER

My French Whore
Kiss Me Like a Stranger

GENE WILDER

the woman who wouldn't

ST. MARTIN'S GRIFFIN ❦ NEW YORK

*To Anton Chekhov, whose short stories
were my inspiration to get to the heart of things*

THE WOMAN WHO WOULDN'T. Copyright © 2008 by Gene Wilder. All rights reserved. Printed in the United States of America. For information, address St. Martin's Press, 175 Fifth Avenue, New York, N.Y. 10010.

www.stmartins.com

Book design by Jonathan Bennett

The Library of Congress has catalogued the hardcover edition as follows:

Wilder, Gene, 1935–
    The woman who wouldn't / Gene Wilder.—1st ed.
       p.cm.
    ISBN-13: 978-0-312-37578-2
    ISBN-10: 0-312-37578-6
    1. Violinists—Fiction. 2. Neurasthenia—Fiction. 3. Sanatoriums—Fiction.
4. Germany—History—1871–1918—Fiction. I. Title.
    PS3623.I5384 W66 2008
    013'.6   dc22

                                                          2007047029

ISBN-13: 978-0-312-54149-1 (pbk.)
ISBN-10: 0-312-54149-X (pbk.)

First St. Martin's Griffin Edition: March 2009

10 9 8 7 6 5 4 3 2 1

When we do something completely out of our control, I think it's a good thing . . . perhaps something worthwhile wants to come out, if only it knew how.

—*Anton Chekhov*

the woman
who wouldn't

ONE

IT SEEMS THAT THE MORE UNBELIEVABLE A STORY is, the more I'm able to believe it.

I'm thirty-three years old. In 1903 I had a nervous breakdown and was sent to a neuropsychiatric hospital wrapped in a straitjacket. How that came about is still hazy, but I'll tell you what I remember.

I'm a concert violinist; at least I was before the breakdown. In May of 1903 I was in Cleveland, Ohio, playing Tchaikovsky's Violin Concerto in D Major, when—right in the middle of the cadenza I had been working on for weeks—I suddenly put my violin down and began tearing up the first violinist's sheet music. I tore his score into small pieces as fast as I could, poured water into the large mouth of a tuba, pounded on the keys of the piano with my fists—only the black keys—and then sat on the floor, weeping. The audience watched all of this with open mouths until security guards rushed in and carried me off the stage.

A few weeks later, after I had calmed down enough to speak three or four sentences in a row that sounded sane, I was interrogated by the chief of the medical staff. The rest of his staff sat in chairs nearby, listening.

"Do you know your name?"

"Jeremy Spencer Webb," I answered.

"Good for you!" the chief doctor said.

"Please don't patronize me."

"I'm sorry," the doctor said quite humbly. "Are you married?"

"No, thank goodness."

"Why do you say that?"

"Because I was married a few years ago and if you had been married to my wife you'd be in a straitjacket now, and I'd be asking *you* questions."

"Is that what caused your breakdown?"

"No, of course not—that's just a bad memory. We're divorced now."

"Do you like your work as a musician, Mr. Webb?"

"I love my work more than I love my life."

"Well then, why did you tear up the other violinist's

musical score . . . and pound the keys of a very expensive Steinway piano with your fist?"

"I don't know. I honestly have no idea."

"Do you have any idea why you poured water into a tuba?"

"I remember thinking that it might be thirsty."

"Are you making a joke, Mr. Webb?"

"No, I'm not making a joke. I wish I were."

The chief of staff stared at me for several seconds.

Two days later I was sent to a health resort in Badenweiler, Germany, which was in the Black Forest, close to the French and Swiss borders. Otto Gross, who was the artistic director of the Cleveland orchestra, wanted my written consent to have me taken there. I was reluctant to give it until he mentioned that the Russian writer Anton Chekhov, who was suffering from consumption, was also at the Badenweiler resort at this time. I had seen a production of Chekhov's play, *Uncle Vanya*, which so intrigued me that I went to the public library in New York and read another play of his, *The Seagull*. I was moved by his insight and exquisite artistry. When Otto Gross also told me that my expenses would be paid by the orchestra, I signed the necessary papers. Just between us, I think they said that they would pay for everything because they were afraid of a possible lawsuit. Sending me from Cleveland, Ohio, to the Black Forest in Germany seemed crazy. Well, who was I to talk?

TWO

I WASN'T ALLOWED TO TRAVEL ALONE, OF COURSE; a young man named Patrick Dunne escorted me. He had a shock of red hair so bright that you could almost see it in the dark. His Irish brogue was very soft, as was his whole manner, but his muscles bulged so large that they showed through his jacket. I knew I would never want to get into a fight with this man.

Patrick traveled with me on the ship to Cherbourg, then by train to Freiburg, Germany, where a Mr. Kreiss was waiting to drive us to the health resort. Mr. Kreiss was Swiss and spoke German, French, Italian, and English, all fluently.

As we drove through the forest, I remember thinking that they probably chose the name "Black" because the trees were so thick at times that the world around us seemed shielded by darkness. When we reached the small village of Badenweiler the view was soft and peaceful and the muscles in my neck began to relax.

Patrick and I got out of the car and followed Mr. Kreiss, who led us to the Sommer Hotel, where most clients of the health spa stayed. It was a cozy-looking place, nestled in a plateau surrounded by purplish green hills. As we walked, the air was cool and pure and I became aware again of how pleasurable it was just to breathe. I could also understand why Anton Chekhov came here to rest, but I doubted if breathing the lovely air, taking warm baths, and walking among the sheep was going to help me understand why I poured water into a tuba, however thirsty it was.

A kind-looking man with a short white beard hurried up to me, calling out:

"Mr. Webb, Mr. Webb—I am Dr. Karl Gross, the manager of this lovely spa, and I'm so happy to meet you."

As we were shaking hands, I asked: "Are you by any chance related to Otto Gross, who runs an orchestra in Cleveland, Ohio?"

"Yes, of course—he is my brother," he said with a

smile. "And Otto made me promise that I would take very good care of you."

The mystery of why I was sent to Germany from Cleveland, Ohio, finally made sense.

THREE

THAT FIRST NIGHT AT THE RESORT A FEW RAIN-
drops were falling, so my guardian and strongman,
Patrick Dunne, ate dinner with me in the simple dining room that held only eleven tables. I was told that
since clients could eat their dinner as early as five
o'clock and as late as nine, the room was never
crowded.

The cheerful French waiter who served us explained
that every client had his or her own schedule for
each day, depending on their treatments, and that for
the "late nighters," both food and drink—including
whiskey and wine—were served in the bistro-style
room next door if it was cold or raining, but that during
these summer months there was also an outdoor café in
the garden, and if the weather was good, a quartet

would play soft music while the clients ate a late supper or had an after dinner drink, or perhaps—he said with a wink—flirted with the new arrivals.

Conversation with Patrick Dunne had not been unpleasant, but it was certainly sparse. I'm sure Patrick had been told exactly what not to talk about—such as giving tubas a drink of water and pounding the black keys of a piano—but he was a nice fellow and I liked him. He said that his father had a metal shop in Dublin and would advertise on the side of horse-drawn wagons, "If Dunne can't do it, it can't be done." I found myself wishing that Patrick were going to stay with me for a while.

THE NEXT morning, when Mr. Kreiss came to take him back to Freiburg to catch his train, I put my arm around Patrick's shoulder and thanked him for getting me to Badenweiler safely. To my great surprise, I had to keep from crying as his car drove away. I felt like a child who was being left alone in a strange place. I also wondered if I were there because I was crazy.

While I was waving good-bye, a tall, thin lady with very short hair, somewhere in her forties I guessed, stood nearby, watching me. When Mr. Kreiss's car was out of sight she walked up and introduced herself as "Gertie" and said she was one of the attendants who worked for Dr. Gross.

"Now we go to work, Mr. Webb, to make you strong and healthy."

Gertie said that she would guide me through my first days of rehabilitation. She escorted me to what looked like a small sport shop where I was fitted with a sweater, walking shoes, and socks, plus a warm jacket. Then we set off on one of "the shorter walks," which was only two miles. The path wound its way through the foothills and small vineyards that surround Baden-weiler. Gertie explained that she wanted to start me out easy and that we would take some "real" walks in a few days.

I had a light supper that evening and went to bed early. I tried to sleep, but I couldn't stop the thoughts. A friend once told me, "Don't try to stop thoughts when you can't sleep—just try to stop words." But the thoughts kept leading to words, such as, "Will I ever be able to play in concerts again? . . . And why in God's name did I pour water into a tuba?"

Early the next morning, Gertie took me on a three-mile walk. We climbed up a fairly steep hill, which felt like a mountain to me, and then we negotiated our way through twenty or thirty sheep on the way down. I kept slipping on the tall grass, which was still moist from the morning dew, but Gertie was always there to pick me up.

That afternoon, after I finished bathing for twenty-five minutes in a large hot bath with five other men, who were also naked, an attendant covered me with a big towel and rushed me into a very cold bath for one minute. Then the attendant wrapped me in a thick white robe and I was allowed to go back to my room, where I shaved, got dressed, and went to what they called the Garden café for tea and scones.

While I was sipping my Earl Grey tea, I heard several gentlemen buzzing like a swarm of bees who had just discovered a new rose. Curiosity urged me to lean in slightly and I learned that the "rose" they were gossiping about was a young woman who had just arrived from Belgium. One of the men—an Englishman—had seen her checking in at the resort and described her as "a cute Belgie," which at first I took offense to, and yet being the flirtatious jerk that I am, I was also intrigued.

My wretched three-year marriage left a stain that I think will last for a lifetime. However, it certainly didn't put me off women—especially if they were young and cute.

FOUR

MY SECOND DINNER ALONE WAS ON A BEAUTIFULLY warm night. I was sitting in the Garden café, sipping some of the local white wine as I waited to order my supper, when in walked a striking young woman. I guessed that she must be the "cute Belgie" that the horny Englishman was referring to. She was alone and, after giving the Garden café a cursory glance, she sat down at the table next to mine. I'm sure her choice of tables had nothing to do with how mature and handsome and eligible I looked, but rather because all the other tables were filled with people who were cheerful, laughing, and gabbing away, except for one table where a woman who looked very ill was trying to mask her face with a napkin so that the rest of us couldn't see she was crying.

Contrary to what the Englishman said to his fellow lechers, the "Belgie" wasn't what I would call cute in the way that a young girl is cute—this was a woman, and she was quite pretty. She was also delicately attractive. She wore a soft lavender dress which had splashes of pink and light blue. She was a little older than the gossipers had led me to believe; I'd say she was twenty-four or twenty-five, very thin, and she had beautiful clear skin. Her hair was a radiant auburn, the kind I had only seen in paintings. I assumed her hair was long because she had it up in a bun at the back of her head. Her mouth wasn't at all inviting. I don't mean that it looked unkind or stern—it was just without the least hint of a smile.

After she sat down at the table next to mine, I took a few more sips of wine, waiting for her to look in my direction, which I knew she would, so that I could give her one of my tender, heart-piercing smiles. But she never looked at me. Not even a glance. I decided to take the initiative.

"Excuse me . . . You seem to be all alone. Would you like to join me at my table?"

"No, I wouldn't," she said.

"Well— Would you like me to join you at your table?" I said with a little laugh.

"No, I wouldn't," she said.

The quickness of her response shut off my spontaneity, so I went back to sipping wine. However, I'm not a quitter—not with women anyway. It's just a question of which button to push. After a minute or two, I turned back to her.

"Excuse me . . . I was very rude just now, not to at least make an introduction. My name is Jeremy Webb. Would you care for a glass of what they call 'Gutedel,' which is the resort's house white wine, taken from the grapes that are grown locally? It's light and delicately scented and very cool and refreshing."

"No, I wouldn't," she answered.

I sat down and took another sip of wine, waited another minute, then turned to her again and pushed another button.

"I'm from America," I said. "I just arrived and I'm a little lonely. I hope I didn't offend you by talking too much."

She turned and stared at me for several seconds. Then she said: "My name is Clara Mulpas, I'm from

Belgium, I'm here because I'm ill, and I don't much feel like talking."

And that was that. I ordered my supper of trout with boiled potatoes and ate slowly, trying not to glance at the attractive Belgian woman. I saw that Clara Mulpas didn't eat; she just drank some herbal tea and left. And she didn't give me so much as a "Good night" or a "Nice meeting you." Just got up and walked away.

LATER THAT night, as I was getting ready for bed, I found that I was slightly angry with Clara Mulpas; angry that my manly charms didn't even come close to piercing her protective armor, or piercing any other part of her for that matter. I found myself wishing that I had said, "Well, good-bye, Clara Mulpas. Nice not knowing you."

IN A way, I learned a great lesson that evening: How could I be stupid enough to continue flirting in my usual manner when I had just had a nervous breakdown? I told myself to forget about women and concentrate on curing whatever was wrong with my brain. "Get back to your violin and forget about women," I told myself. But when I turned out the lights and tried to sleep, I couldn't stop thinking about Clara Mulpas, who had turned me down without so much as a smile. As I was dropping off to sleep I pictured what she would look like with that large bun on the back of her head untied and her long auburn hair lying gently over her thin, naked body . . . next to me.

FIVE

THE NEXT DAY, GERTIE WENT EASY ON ME. I WAS
ordered to get in with the boys for a hot bath, which
was followed by a grapeseed heat pack and a relaxing
grapeseed oil massage. I rested in the sun on a soft
lounge for half an hour—Gertie timed me—then I was
allowed to dress and go to the Garden café for my tea
and scones, which I was eagerly looking forward to because I had only had some fruit juice for breakfast.

I was sitting alone at my table, sipping tea after
eating three delicious scones with clotted cream and
strawberry jam, when I saw a gentleman staring at me
from a table across the room. When he saw that I had
spotted him, he got up and walked toward me. He was
strikingly handsome, in his early forties I would guess,
wearing an immaculate white suit, white shirt, and soft

blue tie. He was also wearing a lorgnette, which I had only seen before when guest conductors came over from Europe. It had a thin black strap that dropped down to the side of his beautifully manicured mustache and goatee. When the gentleman arrived at my table, he smiled.

"Are you the musician Jeremy Webb?"

"Yes, I am."

"My name is Anton Chekhov."

A rush of excitement shot through me. I got up quickly and offered my hand.

"What a great pleasure. I heard that—"

"I can't shake your hand, Mr. Webb," he interrupted. "I'm sorry. I have consumption and I don't want to take even the slightest chance of giving it to you. May I join you?"

"Yes, of course."

After we both sat down, Chekhov said, "Please excuse my bad manners—staring at you from across the room—but I didn't want to disturb you while you were still eating. Dr. Gross told me a little about you and I wanted to meet you and say hello."

"It's a great honor to meet *you*, Mr. Chekhov."

"Why?"

"Well . . . I saw a production of *Uncle Vanya* in New York and was very moved . . . and I read your beautiful play, *The Sea Gull.* But to tell you the truth, when I arrived in Badenweiler, I was a little afraid of meeting you."

"For heaven's sake, why?"

"I get very nervous when I meet people I really respect."

"Why?"

"Well—I hope this doesn't offend you, but—"

"Mr. Webb, I don't offend easily."

"Well, almost all of the people I've idolized from afar—composers and conductors from other countries, mostly—turned out to be very disappointing when I actually met them."

"We're off to a good start. I feel exactly the same way. I hope I don't disappoint you if we have something to drink together. Would you care for a little white wine with me, or would you prefer something stronger?"

"Some white wine would be fine. Thank you."

Chekhov waved to the waiter.

"Two glasses of Gutedel—nice and cold," he said to the waiter. "By the way, have you read any of my short stories, Mr. Webb?"

"No."

"They're much better than my plays. What brings you to this lovely health resort?"

"Oh, well . . . um . . . I had been working very hard, and was very tired, and—"

"Why did you suddenly stop playing the violin in Ohio? Do you have any idea?"

His question caught me completely off guard. I tried to answer intelligently, but nothing intelligent came out.

"That's difficult to— I mean, it's a little embarrassing for me because—I—"

"Was it something to do with the tuba, or the tuba player?" he asked.

I felt drenched with humiliation, afraid that I was going to laugh and cry at the same time.

"Oh, dear. Dr. Gross told you about that. I'm so embarrassed. I'm not quite sure what— I mean how to—"

"Please, don't waste your time being embarrassed— not with me. Forgive me for asking such personal questions, especially on our first meeting. It's just that what happened to you fascinates me, especially giving the tuba a drink of water and pounding only on the black keys of a Steinway piano. It's wonderful! I'm not making fun of you, Mr. Webb—it's just that I wish I could have had the imagination to write these things in one of my stories, instead of hearing that they happened to you."

"So do I."

"Well, don't worry about it. When we do something completely out of our control, I think it's probably a good thing."

"A *good* thing?" I blurted out.

"Yes. Perhaps something worthwhile wants to come out, if only it knew how . . . Don't you think?"

"It's a comforting thought," I said.

The waiter rushed in with our wine. Chekhov raised his glass. "To love!" he said.

"Now why on earth do you say that?" I asked as we clicked glasses.

"Why not?" he said with a tiny smile.

As we both took a sip of wine, I thought, *What a strange bird he is.*

SIX

AN HOUR LATER, DRESSED IN MY LIGHT BLUE SPORT jacket, tan trousers and white shirt, I went to the Garden café where I ordered something called Schwartzwalder Schinken, which Maurice the French waiter said was dry cured ham—a local dish and one of the resort's specialties. As I was sipping a glass of cold Gutedel, smiling as I remembered Chekhov's silly toast "To love," Clara Mulpas walked in.

As she walked toward me, the preposterous thought flashed through my mind that Chekhov was staging this whole thing, as if it were one of his plays. *Hold on now, Jeremy. You're thinking crazy again.*

I made no attempt to sway Clara Mulpas in her choice of tables, but as irony would have it, down she sat at the same table she'd sat at the night before—the one next to me.

When she very casually looked in my direction I made sure not to smile or nod my head in greeting. But this time *she* smiled. The mouth that didn't smile actually smiled at me. So of course, I smiled back. And then the cocky seducer in me took over.

"Good evening Miss Mulpas . . . or is it Mrs. Mulpas?"

"It's Mrs. Mulpas and no, I wouldn't," she said, guessing what my next question was going to be. How infuriating, that she could read me so exactly. I was only going to ask her if she'd like a glass of wine, but I'm sure she knew what was going to come next: "Two lonely people, far from home . . . What a shame that we aren't sitting together, Mrs. Mulpas." She knew a flirt when she saw one. I must give off a scent.

My supper arrived, but before I took even one bite, I suddenly jumped up, stood on the seat of my chair and screamed out to the whole room, "I'M HAVING THE SCHWARTZWALDER SCHINKEN, AND I DON'T CARE WHAT YOU THINK!"

I felt ridiculous and my face was wet with humiliation. After making a complete fool of myself, I sat down as quickly as I could and buried my head into my napkin. *Oh, my God, I really am crazy. I must be. Where did that come from? Now I know how that poor lady must have felt the other night, when she tried to mask her tears behind her napkin.*

To my great surprise, Clara Mulpas called out to me.

"Do you mind if I join you, Mr. Webb?"

"With pleasure, Mrs. Mulpas," I answered, as I quickly wiped the perspiration from my forehead.

I helped her into the chair opposite me and improvised a lie. "Please forgive my outburst, Mrs. Mulpas. I had made a really stupid bet with a friend of mine who said that I would never have the nerve to do such a crazy thing in front of all these people. Forgive me. It was just a childish prank."

"I liked it," she said.

I was stunned.

"I'm tired of people who can't tolerate little pranks, if they're good-hearted pranks," she said. "Or people who can't say what they really think. What was it you told all of us that you were having for dinner? It made me laugh."

"Schwartzwalder Schinken. Sounds funny when you say it in German, but it's really just slow cured ham. Would you like me to order some for you?" I asked.

"No, I'll just have the house salad tonight. I'm not very hungry." She glanced at the waiter, who came quickly.

"Yes, Madame Mulpas," the waiter said. "Ready to order?"

"Je voudrais la salade, encore, Maurice."

"Très bien, Madame."

Then she turned and looked straight at me as she said, "And a glass of Gutedel—nice and cold."

"Of course, Madame."

Maurice left. "You like that little wine?" I asked.

"I had some at lunch. You were right. It's very pleasant. Please don't wait for me, Mr. Webb. Your meal will get cold."

"No, no. It's a room temperature dish. And anyway, I'd prefer to wait for you."

"May I ask what you're occupation is, Mr. Webb?"

"I'm a violinist."

Her face lit up. "Do you mean that you play the violin for a living?" she asked.

"Yes."

"With an orchestra?"

"Very often, yes."

"How wonderful," she said. "Have you ever played in Brussels?"

"Not yet. Is that where you live?"

"Yes."

Maurice arrived with her wine. We raised our glasses.

"Cheers," I said.

"Santé," she said.

As we each took a sip of wine, I purposely did not look "deeply into her eyes," even though I really wanted to.

"What does Mr. Mulpas do?" I asked, using one of my old tricks.

"He runs away from people."

"I'm . . . I don't think I know what you mean, Mrs. Mulpas."

"I mean that when he found out that I had a cancer, he couldn't bear the possibility of living with an invalid, possibly having to take care of her, possibly watching her die, and with no possibility of having children. . . . So he left, weeping, as he packed his things, including his cigars, and walked out. Men are like that, you know. Not all men, of course, but I think most men are."

Unsure of what ground to walk on, I just said, "I see." Clara's salad arrived in time to save me from saying something foolish.

* * *

WHILE I was having coffee and Clara was having her herbal tea, three ladies and one stout gentleman walked in with their instruments—two violins, a viola, and a cello for the gentleman. They made their way to a small gazebo, gave a polite nod to the audience, and began tuning their instruments. When they were satisfied, the first violinist made a little motion with her head, and they all began playing Mozart's String Quartet in D Minor, in perfect harmony.

Clara Mulpas watched me smile as I watched them play. "Tell me why you're smiling, Mr. Webb?"

"It's just that I've played this piece several times. This quartet plays together beautifully."

We talked quietly for almost an hour. I didn't flirt. I was tempted to, of course, but I didn't. Like Chekhov, Clara Mulpas was straight to the point with everything she said. I didn't tell her about my breakdown in Ohio—I wasn't as brave as Clara.

"Why are you here alone, Mr. Webb?"

"Well . . . let's see . . . I'm not married, or otherwise engaged," I said, hoping she wouldn't catch the flirt at work.

"Why aren't you married or otherwise engaged?" she asked, very seriously.

"I *was* married, for the most miserable three years of my life, and that turned me off of marriage for good, I'm afraid."

"Don't waste your time being afraid, Jeremy. Fall in love before it's too late—it's healthier for you. And for your work, don't you think?"

"Perhaps," I answered. "Doesn't your advice apply to you as well?"

"It would have—but it's a little late for me," she said with a cheerful smile that didn't in any way ask for pity.

She stared at me for half a minute. When the clock chimed ten o'clock she got up and said, "Have a pleasant evening, Jeremy. I hope to hear you play the violin one day." And she left.

I finished my glass of Gutedel and went back to my room.

My desires were getting mixed up. Still attracted to Clara Mulpas? Yes, of course, even more than before. But making love with a pretty young woman who doesn't take it at all seriously, only for pleasure, a little fun for a few days, a week, a night . . . Yes! But hugging

Clara's very thin, naked body would be quite different. She is someone who would not be doing it for "a night of fun," who not only listens to you but also hears what you're saying, who is deeply honest about everything she says and who might just fall in love with all of your womanizing hogwash. . . . Well, that's a different world, a much more serious world, and not one that I wished to enter.

Later that night, I fell asleep remembering the thin veil of perspiration on Clara's forehead, and how sensuous it was.

SEVEN

"HOW DO THE CRITICS TREAT YOU, MR. WEBB?"
Chekhov asked while we were having tea the next afternoon.

"Usually very well . . . very respectful . . ."

Chekhov stared at me with his penetrating eyes, giving me a chance to continue. But when he saw that I
was lost in thought, he said, "Except?"

"Pardon me?" I asked.

"They were very respectful, except . . . ?"

My cheeks felt hot. I finally spoke. "I was playing
the Mendelssohn violin concerto in New York and . . .
the next morning . . . the dean of the New York music critics wrote something like . . . um . . . let me see
if I—"

"I'm sure you remember the exact words, Mr. Webb."

"The critic wrote, 'Mr. Webb's violin playing is exceptional on a technical level, but is completely without emotional reality. He knows how to play louder and softer, faster and slower, but nothing else.'"

Chekhov looked at me very kindly. "Even if you don't think you're bothered by what you read in that newspaper, Jeremy, somewhere inside your brain it must tear you apart. Don't you think?"

I nodded a polite yes. I thought it was kind of him to call me by my first name.

"For twenty-five years I've read criticisms of my stories and plays and I don't remember one word of intelligent advice. One time, a critic said something which made an impression on me—he said I would die in a ditch, drunk." Chekhov started laughing. Then he started coughing.

"Excuse me, Jeremy," he said as he got up and left the room.

I wanted to help him, but couldn't. I hate the feeling of being helpless.

That evening, as I was shaving and preparing to go to the Garden café for supper, I thought about Chekhov's words and wondered if I understood any more about why I poured water into a tuba or tore up the first violinist's musical score or pounded on the black keys of a beautiful Steinway piano. It still made no sense to me.

EIGHT

CLIMBING HILLS WAS NEVER ONE OF MY GREAT AM-
bitions. Perhaps I was just lazy, but I admit—now that
I've been climbing a hill every other day—that it's very
difficult to think about the stresses in your life while
you're trying to avoid falling backwards when a goat
with large horns is chasing you because you came too
close to the little patch of grass he was planning to eat
for breakfast. When I finally made it down the hill and
saw the resort, all I could think about was a hot bath
with the boys and then a nice pot of Earl Grey tea with
some scones.

That evening, I was a little nervous about seeing
Clara again. I even imagined the unlikely possibility of
an intimate relationship with her, if only I could find
a way to overcome her very definite "No, I wouldn't"

response. I sat down in the Garden café, ordered some Gutedel, and watched for her as the café began to fill up.

When Clara arrived I thought her appearance had changed slightly. Not suddenly more beautiful or anything as romantic as that; she just seemed weaker, even though the dress she wore was much more colorful than the other two dresses I had seen her in. This dress was mostly crimson red with sprinkles of foam green, and was almost in perfect contrast to her very pale face.

I didn't make the masculine assumption that she would want to sit with me again, now that we were such friendly acquaintances. I gave her a pleasant smile as she came near and I didn't prepare any questions in my mind that started with the words, "Would you?"

To my great surprise, Clara came straight to my table and waited for me to pull out a chair.

"Good evening, Jeremy."

"Good evening, Clara."

There's something to this forthrightness business. It's refreshing.

"Do you think they'll have music tonight?" Clara asked with the eagerness of a child.

"It's such a beautiful night, I'm sure they will. May I ask how you're feeling, Clara?"

"Fine, thank you," she said with a sincere smile, which I didn't believe for a minute.

"Shall we have some Gutedel?" she asked. "It seems to work wonders on my whole disposition. It even takes away headaches. Oh, here they come!"

The musicians walked in, but tonight there were only three of them. They made a little nod to the guests and then the stout man who played the cello stepped forward and said in his slightly German accent: "Ladies and gentlemen, how nice again to see you. But I have a little sorry news. Our first violinist, Madame Denise Chobrier, is home with sore throat, *but*—I have her violin case right here . . . and we also have a famous violinist right here . . . and if it is not a bad imposition, would you please play something with us, Mr. Jeremy Webb from America?"

He pointed to me, the guests applauded, and my heart pounded violently. This wouldn't have bothered me in the least before the horrible incident in Cleveland, but the fear that I would become a lunatic again, and do God knows what, filled me with terror.

I looked at Clara, who seemed thrilled at the lovely surprise.

"Would you like— I mean— Do you want me to play something with them, Clara?"

"Oh yes, very much."

I got up and joined the musicians, for which I was applauded again. The three musicians and I talked for a minute or two about what we should play and what music they had in their books. I asked if they had Schumann's Quartet in E Flat or the Borodin Quartet No. 2. The cellist said, "We all love the Borodin, Mr. Webb; it's so romantic and we have the music for it."

While they were turning the pages of their music books, I made a short speech to the audience.

"Ladies and gentlemen, please don't throw tomatoes if we don't all play together on every note"—the audience laughed—"but we'll try our best. This is the Borodin String Quartet Number Two."

I sat down in Madame Chobrier's chair, took the violin out of her case, and tested my "A" note against the other musicians'. I looked at the first page of music for a few seconds, most of which I remembered, then looked up at my compatriots, gave a slight nod of my head, and we all began playing, in perfect time. The sound was beautiful. So far so good! When there was a slight pause in my part, I glanced quickly at Clara, who seemed enthralled.

I started to become confident that everything was going to go smoothly, when—don't ask me why—I took my violin bow and started bowing my head, and yet my left hand kept fingering the proper strings. I'm sure the audience must have thought that I had an itch on my forehead or scalp or something like that. No one seemed terribly alarmed by my action—until I started bowing my ear. Now the audience was confused. The other musicians continued playing their parts but I saw complete bewilderment on their faces.

During the next pause in my part, I quickly wiped the perspiration from my forehead and looked out at the audience. I saw Dr. Gross, sitting stone faced at his table. Next to him, in his immaculate white suit, was Anton Chekhov. My fear was that they were thinking, "Yes, this poor fellow really is crazy."

On my next cue, I started in time with the others and thought that perhaps the crisis was over, when—with absolutely no premeditation—I started bowing my teeth, and yet my left hand kept fingering the strings in perfect time. Laughter burst out from the guests. I'm sure they thought that this was all planned beforehand as a little comedy act. But Dr. Gross wasn't laughing. I couldn't stop glancing at him as I tried to concentrate. I told myself that he was pulling for me, urging my psyche to get rid of whatever demon was making me do these ridiculous things. Perhaps it was Karl Gross's inspiration, but from then on I played fairly well and in harmony with the other musicians.

When we finished the piece the audience applauded enthusiastically.

"What a treat!" I heard a lady call out.

"Bravo!" a man shouted from a nearby table.

I tried to smile, as if to say, "I hope you enjoyed our little show." But I didn't have the nerve to look at my three fellow musicians. They were dumbfounded.

When I returned to my table I felt like a little dog that had made a mess on the floor and was afraid of being punished. Clara wasn't smiling but she wasn't grim either. There was just a question mark on her face.

"Did you plan all of those funny things beforehand, Jeremy?"

"Well, no, it was—well, just spontaneous," I said, trying to make it sound like it was the silly act of a clown instead of a lunatic.

"But why? The music was so lovely."

"I know, Clara, but . . . *ooph,* it's so difficult to explain. I went too far, I know, but some of these people have suffered so much with their illnesses, and I . . . something came over me and I just wanted to give them a good laugh as well as some good music."

Clara looked at me with her beautiful cerulean blue eyes, in which I could read one simple word: LIAR!

I hardly slept that night, except for one horrible nightmare: I was in a straitjacket. All the patients in the hospital were laughing and throwing tomatoes at me. Some of the tomatoes hit me in the face. Then a very kind-looking, elderly doctor with a soft white beard took my violin out of its case, and showed it to me. As he smashed my violin over a chair, breaking it in half, he said, "Please forgive."

NINE

WHEN I GOT UP THE NEXT MORNING I DECIDED TO get the stifling anger off my chest. I was heading for Dr. Gross's office when I saw Chekhov walking at a fast pace nearby. He looked comical because he was wearing a beautifully pressed tan suit, clean white shirt, blue tie, and a wide-brimmed tan hat, but he was carrying a tackle box in one hand and a fishing rod in the other. When he saw me he gave a slight smile and a polite "hello," but he kept on walking.

I jogged quickly to catch up with him. I asked if he knew whether it had been planned beforehand to have the missing violinist, Madame Chobrier, stay at home so that I would have to take her place.

"I know nothing except that Karl Gross asked me to have supper with him last night."

"Did you come up to my table on the day we met because Dr. Gross asked you to talk with me?"

"I wanted to meet you because I heard that you're a famous musician and I love music. I also love fishing and an abundance of young ladies," he said with a soft smile, "but my love of music was the reason I wanted to meet you."

"And what did you think of my unique performance last night?" I asked as I tried to keep pace with him.

"I thought you were terribly afraid of something," he said. "What did your pretty lady friend think of your performance?"

"I told her that I did all of those crazy things for the sake of the guests who were ill and who needed a good laugh, but she knew I was lying."

"I like her," he said.

"Excuse my American audacity, but have you ever been terribly afraid of anything, Mr. Chekhov—I mean as an adult?"

Chekhov stopped walking and looked at me.

"I'm always afraid of being alone, Jeremy—and I live in terror of going bald."

"Now you're making fun of me."

"I assure you I'm not. Now please excuse me. I have

an important rendezvous with a striped bass. I intend to invite him over for dinner tonight," he said. I stopped walking and watched Chekhov head toward a small lake that I could now see was only about five hundred yards away.

I TOLD Dr. Gross that I believe I saw him in my nightmare and told him what he did to my violin and that the other patients were throwing tomatoes at me. He was silent for a while, and then looked at me without the usual, tender smile on his face.

"Oh, Mr. Webb, I promise you that I never do things to patients for my own amusement. Always there is a reason. Last night I only wanted to see if playing the violin again, in front of a very small audience, would cause you trouble. Which of course it did."

"Can you tell me what my nightmare means?"

"I think you are very afraid that you won't be able to play your violin. That's all. But you will, Jeremy. I promise."

His sweet smile returned. "Please forgive me," he said.

I did forgive him, both to his face and also in my heart, now that I understood. We shook hands warmly and I was about to leave, when I stopped in his doorway.

"Dr. Gross, is Mrs. Mulpas well enough to go on a walk with me one of these days?"

"If you can get her to go, I would dance a jig."

TEN

I WAITED IN THE GARDEN CAFÉ TILL ALMOST EIGHT-thirty before ordering my supper, and then Clara walked in. She looked even more pale than the night before, but she was wearing a lovely rose-colored dress and she had a small pink ribbon in her hair, which I think spoke something of her spirit.

I didn't have to ask her to sit with me; she came right to my table and waited for me to help her into "her chair." After we both sat down, she said, "Today was a little difficult. I hope you weren't waiting for me to eat."

"I wasn't hungry yet. Now I'm famished."

"You're a good liar, Jeremy. What did you order to-night—the Schinkenshwarzensomethingorother again?"

"No, just the baby chicken, with some steamed potatoes and spinach."

"Um, that sounds wonderful. Was the Gutedel nice
and cold, the way you like?"

"It was. Are you ready for some?"

"Oh, yes."

Maurice, who was becoming our friend, came rush-
ing over before I could wave.

"Madame!"

"Pour moi, le poussin, aussi, Maurice."

"Très bien, Madame. Et le Gutedel—nice and cold?"

"Yes," she said with a smile in my direction.

When Maurice left, Clara said, "You have him nicely
trained, I see."

"He's a fast learner. Now then, Clara, let's get down
to some serious business. Would you take a walk with
me, one of these days, if the weather is good, which it
always is . . . and if I'm very polite, which I will be?
And please notice that I didn't say, 'Would you *like?*'
because I don't want to hear another one of your 'No, I
wouldn'ts.' "

"Thank you, Jeremy, but that's something I would
have to talk over with Dr. Gross."

"I already have. He said yes. He also said that he would do a jig if I could get you to go."

She looked away so seriously, as if she were trying to decide the fate of her whole life.

"All right . . . I would like."

ELEVEN

OUR FIRST RENDEZVOUS

The next day Clara and I took our first walk together. The weather was calm and fine; not too warm, but cool enough to enjoy the air. Clara wore a light sweater over her dress. One of the walking paths I was told about wound its way along the small lake called "Mummelsee."

Now, I'm a flirt and I can't say that I'm ashamed of it, but as attracted as I was to Clara, I was very careful. I didn't want her instincts yelling out, "Here it comes—be careful!" So I gave myself these rules: no hand holding and no disguised flirting—like casually slipping my arm around her waist as we walked— because she'd see right through me. So I only held her hand or arm or waist if she happened to stumble on a rock or a branch or a hole in the earth, and in those cases, I admit, I would hold on a few seconds longer than was actually necessary. I couldn't help it—that's the way I am.

When a deer crossed our path, Clara was momentarily startled. I grabbed her hand.

"She's more afraid of us than you are of her, Clara. I promise."

"I'm sorry. It's just that it took me by surprise. We don't have many deer in Brussels."

"Oh look!" I said, still holding her hand. "Do you see her two fawns waiting for their mother?"

We stopped for a moment and watched the fawns disappear into the woods, following their mama. Clara did not pull her hand away.

"They're so beautiful," she said.

As we continued our walk along the lake, Clara continued to hold my hand. We saw a group of young boys splashing each other in the shallow water, playing in the same way that I remembered playing when I was a young boy, swimming in the lakes in Wisconsin with my twelve- and thirteen-year-old friends, whose voices were changing from soprano to tenor. We all practiced swaying our hips from side to side, trying to prove how close we were to sexual manhood, although we wouldn't have known to call it that.

Clara was fascinated by a group of ducks who were waddling between the green pods and weeds along the shore, dunking their heads suddenly when they thought they saw a tasty bit of lunch in the dark water. Then Clara stopped walking.

"Just want to catch my breath, Jeremy. It's beautiful here. Thank you for asking me, but I think I'd better go back now."

So ended our first little rendezvous.

Well, what did I expect—a conquest? *Not yet, Casanova. Not yet.*

TWELVE

I SPENT THE AFTERNOON IN A MINERAL SPRING, followed by a pleasant massage, a shower, and then was off to the Garden café for my tea and scones. There was Chekhov, sitting alone, as always, drinking some strange white concoction. He waved me over.

"Won't you have your tea and scones with me, Jeremy? Why should we both be alone?"

"What in the world are you drinking?" I asked as I sat down.

"It's called koumiss. It's fermented mare's milk, which is supposed to be a source of good bacilli, and I'm supposed to drink four bottles of this unpleasant swill every day. Would you like to try some?" he said with a smile.

"Thank you, no. I don't want to appear rude, but I'm

not sure what I should call you anymore. I feel silly always saying 'Mr. Chekhov,' like a schoolboy, but your culture is so different from mine."

"Why not call me Anton?"

"You don't mind?"

"If I can call you Jeremy, why shouldn't you call me Anton? Unless you prefer Anton Pavlovic?"

"No, no. Anton is fine."

The waiter came over and, knowing very well what I always had in the afternoons, he set hot tea and scones in front of me.

"Did you catch your striped bass yesterday, Anton?"

"Yes, I did. The two of us had a lovely dinner together. I'm sorry I ran away from you so quickly, but I wanted to get my line in the water before the sun became too bright."

Then, from out of nowhere, Chekhov said, "Speaking of critics, Jeremy, are you familiar with Tolstoy?"

"Leo Tolstoy?"

"There's only one Tolstoy. I wasn't there when he came to see *Uncle Vanya,* but I asked a friend, who was with him that night, what Tolstoy thought of my play. I asked him to tell me the absolute truth. My friend hemmed and hawed for a while and then said, 'Tolstoy hadn't understood the play and he thought you were an appalling playwright, but not as bad as Shakespeare.' "

Chekhov laughed and took another swallow of his mare's milk.

"Instead of going off in a corner and sulking, I found it hilarious," he said.

"And you want me to just laugh at the New York critic who thought my violin playing had no real feeling?"

"If I can take it from Tolstoy, you can take it from an egotistical critic who is probably more interested in his clever words than in your violin playing. He probably won't even be there in a year or two. Don't let your tea get cold, Jeremy."

THIRTEEN

THAT NIGHT, CLARA SHOWED UP A FEW MINUTES after eight. She looked better than when I had left her after our morning walk. I thought she had more color in her cheeks, perhaps from the sun, and she looked prettier than ever. I wondered how many dresses she'd brought with her from Brussels because she always came into the café in what looked like a new dress. Well, I supposed there might be a shop somewhere in the village. Who knows? Tonight's dress was soft yellow mixed with little bits of blue.

"What shall we eat tonight, Jeremy?" she asked, slightly out of breath, which I thought was because she might have walked too fast, not wanting to keep me waiting. But that sounds too conceited.

"I think our walk made me hungry," she said.

"Good! I'm starving too. Maurice says we should try the moist smoked ham with herbed sauerkraut and potatoes . . . and he suggests that we have a little white asparagus on the side, while it's still in season."

"Oh, my! Can we share? I mean one order for two? Because I'll never be able to eat a whole portion by myself, Jeremy. But that might not be enough for you?"

"It will be, I promise. I had an extra scone at tea."

The four musicians walked in. I had been waiting for them and I was prepared.

"Excuse me for one minute, Clara. I want to apologize to the musicians for my behavior last night."

I went up to each musician, including Madame Choprier, and laid it on thick. I told them I had lost my head—which of course was true—but I repeated the lie that I told Clara, that I just wanted to give the clients a little laugh. The musicians were very gracious, especially the cellist, whose name was Viktor.

Before I left them, I told another lie. I walked up to the first violinist, Madame Choprier, and said: "I hope your sore throat is a little better tonight, Madame." She blushed and looked away, but the other musicians smiled at my joke. They knew that I knew the truth.

When I returned to our table, Clara said she thought

it was very generous of me to apologize to them, but even as she spoke I could see that same question in her eyes: What was the real reason he acted so bizarrely?

We sipped our Gutedel as we listened to a Mozart quartet. When our food arrived, Clara really dug in. I was surprised by how much she ate.

"Clara, how about if you and I have another picnic tomorrow?" Before she could begin to answer, I plowed right on. "The kitchen said they'd be happy to pack us a light lunch—sandwiches or cold chicken, a little fruit and cheese—even some iced Gutedel with two glasses if we like. We'll find a nice flat spot in the foothills, not too far away, spread a blanket, and watch the fawns looking to see if we're going to give them a bite of our food."

Her eyes drifted off to some hidden place again.

"Clara—it's just a picnic. Please, do what you want."

"Will you play for me?" she asked.

Now I was baffled. "Do you mean, play *with* you?" I asked.

"No, play *for* me," she said. "With a violin."

My heart melted when I realized the innocence of her request.

"Yes, if I can find one," I answered.

FOURTEEN

"I NEED A VIOLIN, DR. GROSS."

"Of course you do, my boy."

"No, I mean I need one *now*! Today! Do you know where I can rent one, or buy one?"

Dr. Gross lavished one of his angelic smiles on me. "Do you know of Gerhardt Fleischer, the famous German violinist?"

"No, I'm afraid I don't."

"No, of course not—Fleischer was a little before your time. He was here for several months, Mr. Webb, and he was so ill that I used to beg him to rest more, but he insisted on practicing every single day for three hours . . . until the day before he died. I have his violin, which I have taken good care of. You may borrow it, Mr. Webb, if you promise to take care of it, and not bow your head and teeth," he said with a twinkle in his eyes.

"I promise."

Dr. Gross disappeared for a few minutes and then returned with a violin case. He handed it to me.

"I'll take good care of it, Doctor. Thank you."

As I was walking out of his office, I stopped and said, "Oh, by the way—I think Mrs. Mulpas is getting much better, don't you?"

He looked at me without a smile. "My dear fellow, Mrs. Mulpas is dying."

I stared at him like a wooden puppet.

"Are you absolutely sure?" I asked.

"I had hopes, Mr. Webb. I always have hopes. But the body doesn't lie. She has a cancer in the stomach that we can't remove. The only reason I tell you this information—which of course is very private—is because I know you have a great fondness for Clara, and I don't want you to do anything foolish that might tax her strength too much."

"Does she know?"

"Clara and I talk about everything. She's stronger in the heart than anyone I know. I want her to enjoy herself as much as possible. The pain is going to come later. For now, I tell her—try to rest, eat good food, don't tire your body."

I nodded my head up and down, understanding everything and nothing. We shook hands and I left.

FIFTEEN

OUR SECOND RENDEZVOUS

In my left hand I carried a basket filled with food, knives, forks, wine, and glasses. In my right hand, which is stronger, I carried the violin case. Clara carried a blanket and two small cushions, which the hotel had given us so we wouldn't have to sit on pebbles or branches.

I found a path that the gentleman at Reception told me about. It led into the foothills, but not very far away, and then into the trees. I wanted to find a path that wasn't well known, that other visitors wouldn't be using, so we climbed for about eight or ten minutes into the forest, resting frequently. Each time I stopped I told Clara it was because my arms were getting tired from carrying everything.

We found a tiny plateau of soft grass, surrounded by

trees, which looked ideal. The sun filtered lightly through the branches and leaves, and there was also a small brook that ran nearby.

Clara spread the blanket. I put the basket and violin case down, and we rested for a few moments.

"You've got a worried look in your eyes, Jeremy. Something's wrong, isn't it?"

"Not a bit! I'm just trying to figure out what kind of sandwich I'd like to start with and which piece of music I should play for you. Those are very serious questions—especially which sandwich."

"How do you know what kind of sandwiches they put in?"

"I peeked! Now, music first or eating?"

"Music!" she said, like a little girl, as if it were a birthday present.

I carefully took out Gerhardt Fleischer's violin, bowed across the strings until I was satisfied with the pitch—which I'm very good at because I'm blessed with a perfect ear—and then I played Robert Schumann's very short, very sweet piece called Traumerei, which means dreaming or reverie. As much as I loved this piece and thought how calming it would be for Clara, I also chose it because it was so romantic.

As Clara watched me play I saw her eyes drift off to a heavenly place every once in a while. "Reverie" was right. She looked so calm and happy, and what I had earlier seen as a very pretty lady, I now saw as a beautiful woman.

When I finished playing, I said, "Now let's eat!"

"Jeremy, won't you at least give me time to tell you how beautiful your music was, and how moved I was?"

"All right, go ahead."

"Oh, you silly man! It was beautiful. Thank you."

"Good! Let's eat."

Clara opened our picnic basket and started laying out food while I opened the bottle of Gutedel with a waiter's corkscrew. I chose a ham sandwich with lettuce, tomato, and some kind of pink dressing that smelled wonderful. Clara chose a chicken sandwich. I poured some wine into our glasses, but filled them only halfway, remembering the picnics I used to go on with my family and how often I spilled a glass or bottle of soda when I tried to balance it on a blanket.

"To long life and happiness," I said, regretting the "long life" part after I said it.

"To happiness," she answered, as we clicked glasses.

After I finished my sandwich and Clara finished half

of hers, she started cutting up bits of cheese for us to have with a ripe pear.

"Tell me about your wife," she said, just like that. No leading up to it.

"Well . . . let me see. Two weeks after our marriage, she turned into a witch."

"You mean . . . What do you mean?" she asked. "You don't mean a real witch, do you?"

"Yes, a real witch. She was very pretty and she had beautiful long hands. When we returned from our honeymoon I had to go back to work, but when I came home from rehearsals each night, there was nothing to eat. She wouldn't cook or shop or wash a dish or make the bed. She wouldn't even buy soap for the bathroom, even though I gave her plenty of money and she was free all day."

"Oh dear. But didn't you make love together?"

"Once every six months—like clockwork. I was a faithful husband for three years, but when the sadness of my marriage finally inched its way past my self-pity and into my brain, I got a divorce . . . and I was liberated."

"I see."

"I didn't mean to make you sad, Clara."

"You didn't make me sad. I'm happy you got rid of the witch."

"Would you tell me about your husband, or is that insensitive of me right now?"

"I like insensitive questions—haven't you figured that out yet? Gustav was what, in French, we would call *'un con,'* which means—well, a bad thing. An ass, I think you say in English, but worse than that. He was a big man—not cruel—but weak and dumb and I think he wanted to marry me because I was from a good family and he wanted financial help from my father so he could go into some kind of tool-shop business. And he wanted lots of children. I was a virgin, of course. He would put his willy into my private part and pump. There was no delight for me, or rapture, or any of the things I had heard about when I was growing up—just Gustav pumping up and down until he was finished. Then he would stand up and say, 'Thank you, Clara,' and that was the lovemaking. We did that five times and then I found out that I had a stomach cancer, which my mother and grandmother had also had, and off Gustav ran—weeping, 'I can't, I can't,' as he packed his bags, took his cigars, and left. My father arranged for an annulment shortly after Gustav left.

Clara smiled like a cherub and said, "Sound like fun?"

"I think I'd like another glass of wine."

"Me too," she said, and filled our glasses halfway again.

"To always being honest with each other," she said, as we clicked glasses.

"To honesty," I said, with tightness in my throat.

"I suppose you want to kiss me now," she said, and she was not making a joke.

What an unusual woman. Well, tell her the truth.

"I do want to kiss you, Clara—not because of the story you told me about your asshole husband—but because I've wanted to kiss you since we met."

"I know that. Well then, ask me!" she said, like a schoolteacher.

Don't laugh . . . Don't laugh . . . It's just the way she is.

"Would it be all right if I kissed you, Clara?"

"Yes, it would," she answered.

I put my arm around her waist and gently pressed my lips against hers. At first she kept her eyes open, but after we both lay back onto the blanket, her eyes closed and she folded herself into my shoulder as we had a beautiful, long and tender kiss. And then she fell asleep.

In my former life—which was about two weeks ago—I would have said to myself, *"Good for you, Jeremy. Now gently slip off her skirt while she's still in this dreamy state, and then—"* No! You don't womanize with a dying woman, no matter how desirable and accessible she is. You may be a flirt but you're not a brute. Anyway, she's sleeping—not because of your exquisite kiss, lover boy, but probably because of the wine she drank, and the music, and the excitement of romance, which she's not used to."

I brushed away a fly that looked like it was about to land on Clara's eyelid. *What an angel face she has. I don't want her to die. And I don't want her to fall in love with me on the rebound from that asshole she was married to, or out of vulnerability because of her thoughts of death and cancer. I just want her to be happy, for as many weeks or months or days that she has. The pain is going to come later, Dr. Gross said. Well, watch over her, Jeremy. But I'll be glad when I'm healthy enough to return to my work and my home, without responsibility for Clara's happiness*

* * *

THAT EVENING I received a note addressed to Mr. Webb, from Mrs. Mulpas. It read:

> *Dear Jeremy:*
> *Too tired to eat dinner . . . perhaps because I'm so happy after our lovely picnic. I'll see you tomorrow. I hope you're happy, too.*
>
> > *Clara*

SIXTEEN

THE NEXT MORNING THE SKY WAS FILLED WITH ominous clouds that promised a thunderstorm in a very short while. I was about to call Clara's room when the receptionist handed me another note.

"It's from Mrs. Mulpas, sir," the receptionist said.

> *Because of the coming storm, I am going to be a good girl and do all of my treatments today, just as Dr. Gross wants me to. Perhaps we can have dinner together tonight . . . if you still like me.*
>
> *Clara*

"If you still like me?" I'd never met anyone like her. I went to my room and practiced with Gerhardt Fleischer's violin for a few hours, but from out of nowhere

I became so emotional that I had to stop for a while. When I finished playing, I decided to call Dr. Gross. He said I could come to his office in half an hour.

"I DON'T know what's happening. I'm terribly upset, Dr. Gross, and I think I need—"

"Please—won't you call me Karl?"

"Thank you. And please call me Jeremy."

"Good! Now then, sit down and tell me what seems to be the trouble?"

"I need to know if I'm crazy."

"Of course you're not crazy. I told you that. You just do crazy things."

"But why?"

After quite a long pause, he said, "How was your picnic with Clara?"

"Fine. Very nice. But she's probably told you everything already."

"No, no, not everything. I only know that you made her happy, that's all."

"I don't want to hurt her, Karl. I care for her, and yes, I'm attracted to her. But I don't want marry her or promise her anything or make her fall in love with me or—"

"You don't want to hurt her—I understand that. Don't worry so much. You cannot make that woman do anything she doesn't want to do. Clara is stronger than you or me. You think you're a bad person, but you are a *good* person. . . . Can you possibly live with that, Jeremy?"

"Are you saying that I do crazy things because I can't accept that I'm a good person?"

"No, not at all. *That* would be crazy. I'm talking to you about Clara and you're talking to me about that tuba again and pounding the piano and—by the way, why *did* you pour water into that tuba?"

"I don't know. I really don't. The tuba player in Cleveland was a nice enough man. He was sort of—"

"What was his name?"

"Carlo! Why do you ask?"

"Did you like him?"

"Yes. Everyone liked him, but—"

"But—?"

"Well, Carlo was a little heavy. . . . I mean, quite overweight . . . and the conductor kept picking on him—always referring to him as 'Fatso' in front of the full orchestra. That's a terrible thing to do. I mean, you do have to be fairly big to carry a tuba around."

"Why didn't anyone say anything to the conductor?"

"I did! I said plenty. I told the conductor—in front of the whole orchestra—to shut his fucking mouth or I would shut it for him."

"Good for you! But why did you pour water into Carlo's tuba?"

"I DON'T KNOW! I THOUGHT HE MIGHT BE THIRSTY!"

"Who?"

"CARLO! I mean . . . Oh, my God, what am I talking about? This is crazy."

"Not at all. I'm sure Carlo was very relieved."

"When?"

"When you gave him a glass of water to show that you cared about him."

Karl Gross's angelic eyes seemed to look right into my brain as he gave me one of his devilish smiles.

SEVENTEEN

IT WAS POURING BUCKETS THAT AFTERNOON. I went to the small indoor dining room for my tea and scones and Chekhov motioned me to come over. He was tucked away in a corner, sipping his mare's milk.

"I think it's a stupid habit to ask, 'How are you doing, old fellow?' as the English say. I hate the sound of it. Why don't you just sit down and tell me about food and wine . . . and Mrs. Mulpas."

"What's that brown thing you're eating?" I asked.

"They call it a *'Gesundheit brot,'* meaning a health bread, but it tastes more like a *'Kranken brot,'* so I dabbled a little cinnamon and sugar on it—don't inform on me. Now then, tell me things."

I motioned to Maurice to bring me "my usual."

"I went on a picnic with Mrs. Mulpas."

"Good! I like the sound of it already. Where?"

"To a secluded place in the foothills, not far from here. The chef packed sandwiches for us and a little cheese, and some Gutedel. We even had glasses and a blanket and cushions. It was wonderful."

"This makes me happy, but also a little jealous. May I ask if your romance is at the galloping stage, or are you just trotting?"

"Somewhere in between, I think. I care for her, Anton, but I'm not at all interested in anything permanent, if that's what you're worried about."

"I'm not worried about anything except staying alive. I just can't help relating things to my own life. I was always careful to keep my ladies at a distance and I would break things off if they got too heated. But the irony is—despite all of my stupid philosophizing—I got married two years ago." Chekhov laughed. "This could be one of my plays, you know. Or better yet, a short story."

"But where's your wife? What's her name? I'd like to see her."

"So would I. Her name is Olga Knipper and she's a wonderful actress and wants to come and visit her husband, but it seems that Mr. Stanislavski and his famous

Moscow Art Theatre can't put on even one play without Olga acting in it. And the doctors won't let me go to her right now."

Maurice came in with "my usual."

"Ah, here come your scones. Please, drink your tea and tell me more about your picnic."

"Well, it was a lovely day and—"

"I hope there's a kiss involved. I'm sorry—I shouldn't interrupt. This is your story, not mine. Yes, 'it was a lovely day and'—"

"—and Dr. Gross let me borrow a violin that used to belong to a famous violinist, and before Clara and I ate our lunch I managed to play a short piece by Schumann without doing any of my famous crazy antics. Anyway, Clara liked it very much."

"Which piece did you play?"

"The Traumerei."

"Beautiful. By the way, are you at all familiar with Rachmaninov?"

"He's my favorite," I answered.

"You have good taste. Did you know that when he premiered his first symphony, the critics tore him apart? He suffered a nervous breakdown, contemplated suicide, couldn't write music for almost a year, until he began working with a psychologist who gave him something called 'auto-suggestive therapy.' He recovered his confidence and wrote his Piano Concerto Number 2, which is now being played all over the world. Why don't you take another little bite of that delicious-looking scone with your tea?"

"Dr. Chekhov—are you treating me with auto-suggestive therapy right now?"

"I *was* a doctor, Jeremy. I gave that up several years ago. I'm not a psychiatrist or psychologist, I'm just an artist, like you, but I know a great deal about critics and nervous breakdowns . . . and people who are exploding with anger."

I took another bite of my scone and a sip of tea, but I didn't look at Chekhov when I asked, "And you think I'm exploding with anger because of that son-of-a-bitch music critic from New York?"

"No, not at all. Well—I don't know. My guess is that you're terribly angry with someone else. But what do I know?"

"Anton, do you honestly think I could be that angry with someone else and not even know who that person is?"

"Perhaps. I know that I've been boiling with anger

at one woman or another who disappointed me terribly, but at the time I wouldn't allow myself to know how truly angry I was. I still wanted to protect them, I suppose . . . or didn't want them to stop loving me, or stop thinking kindly of me, or something like that. Life is strange."

Chekhov took another sip of his mare's milk and made a sour face when he took a bite of his *Gesundheit brot.*

"Would you like a little taste of this *Kranken brot,* Jeremy?"

"No, thank you."

EIGHTEEN

SHE FINALLY WORE A DRESS I HAD SEEN ONCE BE-
fore: the lavender with a splash of pink and light blue.
Clara was smiling and she looked exuberant as she
walked toward me. It was still too cool to sit in the garden so we sat in the dining room.

"What are we having tonight?" she asked.

"Lake trout, if that's alright with you?"

"Oh good, I was hoping for some fish. Have you
heard anything about the weather tomorrow?"

"The storm is over. It's supposed to be beautiful."

"Can we have another picnic?" she asked, with the
excitement of a child.

"Of course. But you'd better bring a sweater along,
just in case."

*   *   *

I TRIED to fall asleep that night, but I kept recalling the few times in my life when I was actually "exploding with anger," as Chekhov put it. Apart from one particular memory of my time with the "witch," when I threw my dinner plate, with a sirloin steak, which I had bought and cooked, onto the ceiling—and my memory of that stupid conductor in Cleveland who kept calling Carlo "Fatso"—the only image that kept coming to mind was a woman named Miss Schneider, from Milwaukee, Wisconsin.

When I was twelve and my mother was terribly ill, my father hired a tall, matronly lady named Elsa Schneider to watch over my mother while he was at work. Five afternoons a week. But in those afternoons— while my mother was lying in bed and constantly in pain—Miss Schneider spent most of her time trying to convert her into becoming a Christian Scientist. She tried to get her to give up all her heart medications and to stop seeing her doctor. She also tried to have an affair with my father when he came home. I didn't know about that until much later, but I knew something was wrong when I heard Miss Schneider telling my mother to throw away her medicine and stop seeing her doctor. And yet, Miss Schneider was always so soft-spoken and gentle with my mother, even while she was trying to poison her mind. I felt helpless, because I didn't know what I could do. But my father did. When he came home and my mother told him what was happening, he screamed at Miss Schneider: "ARE YOU CRAZY? ARE YOU NUTS? WHAT THE HELL'S THE MATTER WITH YOU?" And he kicked her out of the house. I wanted to be able to get angry that way. I even went into our basement and pretended that Miss Schneider was standing in front of me, and I shouted: "Are you crazy? Are you nuts? What the hell's the matter with you?" and then I slapped a cushion in the face, as if it were Miss Schneider. But that was all pretend and it was so long ago. I finally fell asleep exhausted.

NINETEEN

OUR THIRD RENDEZVOUS

The next day, the weather was beautiful. After a short walk we found our grassy plateau in the woods. Clara spread the blanket and cushions and took out the food. I took out Gerhardt Fleischer's violin.

"What are you going to play for me today?" she asked.

"Chopin. Please pour yourself a little wine, Clara. I'll have mine later, *if* I play well for you."

I looked at Clara sitting on the blanket, a streak of sunlight resting on her auburn hair, and then I played one of my favorite nocturnes. It was soft, dreamy, and a little sad . . . something like Clara. When I finished, she was crying.

"That was—" She took several sips of wine as she

wiped her tears with a linen napkin. "You can have your wine now, Jeremy."

After I put the violin away, Clara poured a glass of Gutedel for me. I sat down next to her and she raised her glass. "To beautiful music," she said.

We clicked glasses as I repeated, "To beauty," thinking of how beautiful Clara looked just then.

After several more sips of wine, she said, "I suppose you want to lie down with me."

"I . . . I'm not exactly sure what—"

"With clothes on," she said.

"Yes. I'd like that very much," I said.

"Well then, ask me!" she said.

Here we go.

"Would you like . . . me . . . to lie down next to you . . . keeping my clothes on?"

"Yes, I would," she answered.

I lay down beside her and put my arm under her head as she nestled into my shoulder. We stayed that way for several minutes, without talking. There was no attempt on my part to do anything more, even though I wanted to; we simply enjoyed the closeness and the warmth of our bodies. Then, without saying a word, she suddenly lifted her head, leaned over me, gave me a long kiss on the lips, returned to her position on my shoulder, and fell asleep.

She slept for almost thirty minutes and even though my arm throbbed for lack of blood flow, I didn't want to disturb her. When Clara woke with a start, she looked around, as if she were trying to see where she was, and then seemed to recognize me.

"What happened? Oh! I fell asleep, didn't I? I'm not used to drinking wine so early. I'm sorry, Jeremy. Please forgive me."

"Nothing to forgive. I took a little nap, too. But it was nice holding you in my arms. Well, on my arm. You must be hungry, Clara. There's a nice salad that the chef made for you."

While we had lunch, Clara asked me dozens of questions, about Chopin and nocturnes and what an étude was and what was the difference between sharps and flats. And then she wanted to know how I started playing the violin.

"It was my mother. She bought me my first violin when I was five years old. She had wanted to be a concert pianist before she had her first heart attack, but her instinct told her that I would take to the violin more than a piano—don't ask me why—and I'm sure she was right. We didn't have much money, but she coaxed and charmed the best teachers in town to take me on. And you know, when your mother thinks you're good at something, it gives you confidence that you really are good at that thing."

"Is she still alive?"

"No, she died two years ago, but—now stop crying, Clara—she was there when I gave my first concert at Carnegie Hall, and that meant the world to her."

"Oh, good. I'm so glad."

We packed up our things and headed back to the hotel. Clara held on to my arm as we walked. Nothing that special had happened, and yet I was very content with our little rendezvous.

TWENTY

"COULD I ASK A GREAT FAVOR OF YOU, JEREMY?"
Dr. Gross asked.

"Of course," I answered, assuming that his request
had something to do with helping Clara.

"I know that you've been playing the violin for
Clara, and playing it beautifully. Would you play once
more for our guests . . . but no string quartet . . . just
you? And no tricks, I promise. I only want to see if we
are making the progress that I think we are making with
your condition. Or should I say the progress that you
and I and our spa and Clara Mulpas are making with
your condition? But no pressure! Only if you want. If
you are at all worried or uneasy, then please—"

"Does Clara know what you're asking me to do?"

"Of course not. I would never say anything with-out—"

"I'll do it—but don't tell Clara."

That night, a little after eight, Clara came into the Garden café and sat down next to me. I squeezed her hand and said, "Excuse me, Clara," then reached under our table to get the violin case, walked onto the small platform where the quartet had played, and looked at the audience.

Dr. Gross was sitting at his table near the back of the restaurant, smiling a little nervously. Next to him sat Chekhov, with his handsome, noncommittal face.

"Ladies and gentlemen . . . a few nights ago, when I was playing with the string quartet, I think I ruined some very good music with my silly antics. Tonight I'd like to play for you again and try to make up for the last time."

The audience applauded politely. Most of the guests who were still eating put down their silverware and watched me. I took out Gerhardt Fleischer's violin.

"This piece was written by Niccolò Paganini, the fa-mous Italian virtuoso. It's called 'The Caprice Number 24 in A Minor' . . . but I would rename it: 'Look at me—I'm a showoff.' "

The audience laughed with a little more enthusiasm.

"The twenty-fourth caprice has come close to driving some violinists mad, but since that's already happened to me, I'm not at all afraid."

The audience laughed again, even more cheerfully. Karl Gross smiled. Even the corners of Chekhov's mouth curled up slightly.

I felt the confidence that comes with musical familiarity, because I've played this piece many times as an encore. I tucked the violin under my chin, took a deep breath, and began playing. As insanely difficult as the Caprice No. 24 is, I poured my heart into it and it was coming out pretty well, despite the fact that I hadn't played it for more than a month. While I was playing, thoughts ran in and out: *When will the crazy man appear? How long before I ruin this piece of music?* After slightly more than five minutes, I flew over the mountains and landed safely. The audience rose in unison to applaud me.

I looked at Clara, who was beaming. I lifted my shoulders as if to ask, "Was I all right?" She nodded a sweet yes.

The audience wouldn't stop applauding. I urged them to sit back down.

"I'll play just one more selection for you. It's very soft, very romantic and, I think, a little mysterious. I dedicate it to Clara Mulpas, who is very much like this piece of music. It's called 'Songs My Mother Taught Me.'"

I played Dvorak's short, simple song and when I finished, the audience applauded warmly. When I looked at Clara, I saw tears streaming down her face. I put the violin back into its case and walked back to our table.

"Now I could eat a horse," I said. "Well, no— perhaps a cow or a chicken."

"Can we have a picnic tomorrow?" Clara asked, while patting her wet cheeks with a napkin.

"Of course! Why do you think I chose that song?"

LYING IN bed that night I had another little conversation with myself: *You knew she would love "Songs My Mother Taught Me" and that she would cry, but did you have to say it was soft and romantic, like her? That's the seducer working—don't you know that?* YES, I KNOW THAT, AND I WAS AWARE OF IT AT THE TIME. NOW SHUT UP AND GO TO SLEEP!

TWENTY-ONE

OUR FOURTH RENDEZVOUS

Knowing Clara's predilections by now, the chef made us a beautiful Salade Niçoise: tomatoes, tuna, hardboiled eggs, boiled potatoes, a variety of lettuces, all topped with a light vinaigrette, no anchovies. We each had a glass of Gutedel.

Clara kept staring at me while we ate, hardly speaking, which wasn't like her. When we finished as much as we were going to eat, she glanced up a few feet above her head.

"Did you notice those two dragonflies that were circling above us?" she asked.

"I did. They seemed very playful."

"Did you know that dragonflies make love while they're in flight?"

"Are you making a joke, Clara?"

"No."

"Well, that must be very difficult to manage while they're flying?"

"I suppose you'd like to see me naked now."

My God, this is an unusual woman.

"Yes, I would," I answered.

"Well then, ask me."

Here we go.

"Clara . . . would you like . . . to take off your clothes . . . so that I can see you naked?"

"Yes, I would," she replied, and started undressing. Then her head popped up. "Aren't you going to take off your clothes, too?"

"Yes, of course."

When we were both naked, we lay on the blanket and I embraced her, but very gently.

"Now what do we do?" she asked, without the slightest hint of a smile. "My only experience was with Gustav, who just stuck his willy into my private part and pumped me."

"Let's lie quietly for a few moments and let me kiss you," I said.

I kissed her cheeks and then her lips. When I kissed her breast, she let out a small squeal.

"No, don't stop!" she said. "I was just surprised. Gustav never touched me there. He never touched me anywhere, really."

I kissed both of her breasts and she stroked my hair.

"Am I allowed to touch your willy?" she asked.

"Of course," I said.

She very lightly took hold of my penis.

"My—it's not what I imagined," she said. "I like touching it."

I touched what she called her private part.

"Oh goodness . . . Oh goodness . . . Please don't stop. I was always so dry when Gustave pumped me. Please don't stop."

I gently put my penis into her vagina. When I did, she let out a loud moan, and then pulled my neck down to her chest so that she could kiss me. When our lips touched, her tears flowed like gentle raindrops, her body went limp, and she fell asleep in my arms.

Well? . . . This is what you've been planning and flirting for, isn't it? Are you happy? No attachments—just a lovely girl who's going to die, so there's nothing to worry about.

You'll make a nice excuse: "I have to leave town for a while, dear . . . please take care of yourself . . . think of me . . . I'll write."

Look at her sleeping like a child. What's wrong with giving her a small taste of sexual happiness for the first time in her life? Wouldn't that be a good thing? . . . A small blessing? . . . Something that she would wish for, even ask me for, which she did, even though she knew she was dying? Or am I just rationalizing my cheap, sexual desire? I'm tired of all these battles with myself. I still think I'm a good person.

When she woke, I said, "I think you'd better cover up, Clara. I don't want to be responsible for your catching a cold. What would Dr. Gross say?"

"He'd say, 'Are you happy, Clara, dear?' And I'd say, 'Yes I am, Karl.'"

"Well, cover up anyway—the deer in this neighborhood are starting to talk."

Clara stood up and kissed me; then she got dressed.

THAT NIGHT, Clara and I had a wonderful dinner together. She looked more exultant than ever, and the dress she wore was another one I hadn't seen. Usually, Clara was a slow, very deliberate talker, but tonight she jabbered away like one of the cow birds in the trees above us. At one point she talked so fast that she almost choked on her words. She put her napkin to her mouth, coughed for several seconds, wiped her mouth, and then went on with her story, but I saw the red drops of blood on her napkin.

TWENTY-TWO

I WENT TO SEE DR. GROSS THE NEXT MORNING.

"The blood you saw was coming from the cancer in her stomach, and I'm afraid it's going to get worse."

"May I ask if Clara has told you anything about our relationship, Karl?"

"She tells me little things, Jeremy, but she doesn't tell me *every* little thing. I do know that she seems to be happier now than she has been since I met her. But I think, perhaps, you know more about that than I do."

"Karl, I love being with Clara, but I think she feels more for me than I anticipated. When I met her I thought she was a strong, cool, haughty, even aloof woman. Now I see how fragile she is, and I'm terribly afraid of hurting her."

"My dear young man, Clara has been hurt so much

by life before she ever met you, and I'm afraid she's going to be hurt again, no matter what you do and no matter when you leave—which I'm sure is what you're asking me. But you've already made her happy, Jeremy. . . . by the attention you pay to her, and your tenderness . . . and making her feel like a woman. You don't need to feel guilty."

"I mean no disrespect, Karl . . . but do you ever consult with other doctors?"

"Yes, of course. I'm taking her to Geneva tomorrow to see my friend, Dr. Joseph Hartmann, who is a specialist in her kind of cancer. He is a younger man. . . . Maybe he'll see something that I don't see. Anyway, I always have hopes."

TWENTY-THREE

THE NEXT MORNING, MR. KREISS—THE SAME driver who picked up Patrick and me in Freiberg and drove us to Badenweiler—arrived at exactly seven-thirty A.M. Now he was taking Clara and Dr. Gross to Freiberg to catch the train to Geneva. I shook hands with Mr. Kreiss when he got out of his auto. "Are you going with us, Mr. Webb?" he asked.

"No, I just want to say good-bye to my friends." What I didn't say to Mr. Kreiss was that I might never see Clara again.

Clara was wearing a jacket over her dress and Karl Gross was in a lightweight tan suit. Mr. Kreiss took both their bags and put them in the trunk. I shook hands with Karl, who even gave me a hug. Then I moved close to Clara—who was crying, of course.

"No, no, no," I said, as I wiped some tears from her face. "You're the woman who wouldn't even talk to me when we met, remember? . . . Except for saying, 'No, I wouldn't,' every time I asked you a sweet, endearing little question."

"You were flirting with me," she said, and then she let out a girlish giggle.

"Well, it worked, didn't it?"

She looked up at me without a smile. It was a frightened look. I took her face in my hands and kissed her. Then I kissed her again.

"We'd better go now or we miss the train," Mr. Kreiss said politely but quite authoritatively.

"Yes," Dr. Gross said. "In we go, Clara."

He helped Clara into the car and put a blanket over her lap. She looked out at me. I put on a big smile.

Hold on . . . Hold on . . . You'll be free in two minutes. No more fighting with yourself. No more guilt. Write to her often at first and then keep in touch with Karl, to find out how she's doing. You couldn't go through what she's going through—not as courageously, that's for sure. Well, keep a smile on your face, Jeremy. . . . Make her think it's just a few days before we'll have another picnic. Wave good-bye when the car pulls away. . . . Throw her a happy kiss. . . . Hold on . . .

Karl was about to get into the car, when I suddenly pulled him back and jumped onto the seat beside Clara.

"You don't mind if I go along, do you, Clara?"

Tears and laughter. Karl got into the car and joined in with the laughter.

"You can leave now, Mr. Kreiss," I said.

"Are you sure, Jeremy?" Clara asked.

"Yes, I'm sure—but I need to buy a toothbrush somewhere."

TWENTY-FOUR

GENEVA WAS A BEAUTIFUL CITY, SO CLEAN AND white that you'd think a crew had just scrubbed it down with soap and brushes for our arrival. The hotel that Mr. Kreiss drove us to—the Grand Excelsior— was a beautiful structure with classical columns near the entrance and sculptured moldings around each window. The Excelsior was only a few hundred feet from Lake Geneva.

I was afraid the hotel might not have a room for me, because of my last-minute impulse, but when the registrar saw Dr. Gross, he came out from behind his desk, almost bouncing and making a little humming sound as he walked up to him. They shook hands like old friends. Clara and the registrar spoke in French for half a minute and then the registrar shook hands with me.

I was given a nice room on the third floor, just a few doors away from Clara's room on one side and Dr. Gross's on the other. It had a soft bed and a terrace that overlooked Lake Geneva.

Clara had an appointment at three-thirty that afternoon, at the University Hospital, with Dr. Hartmann, the specialist. I asked Karl if I could come along, but he thought it would be better if I waited. He wanted to keep Clara as calm as possible.

I felt a terrible anxiety after Clara left for her appointment. My body felt warm and my forehead and palms were cold. After all the talk of hospitals and doctors and medications, and some kind of a scope that would be pushed down Clara's throat and into her stomach, I began to fully realize the complications of my attachment to Clara.

I decided to take a stroll along the walkway that bordered the lake. It was still light outside, and although the weather was cool, it was very pleasant.

As I walked, Chekhov's voice shoved itself into my thoughts. *"I was always careful to keep my ladies at a distance. If it got too heated, I would break things off."*

Yes, Anton. Easier said than done.

The blue water of Lake Geneva looked clean enough

to drink, and I wanted to drink it. I had the urge to run into the lake with my clothes on and splash around, as if I didn't have a care in the world. Fortunately, it dawned on me that *that* would be crazy.

I thought it was very civilized that most of the shops in Geneva remained open till seven in the evening. After cashing a few of my Thomas Cook travelers checks—which I had packed into my wallet before leaving Ohio—I bought a white shirt, a tie, two pair of socks, two pair of undershorts, a razor, and a toothbrush. And, just in case I didn't like the taste of the toothpaste that was provided in my bathroom, I bought a tube of toothpaste called *Menthe poivrée,* which I hoped meant peppermint. I put the items in a large cloth bag that cost three francs.

I passed a pastry shop as I was walking. In the window I saw delicious-looking cakes, pies, cookies, and assorted sweets that I knew would make Clara's mouth water. What a stupid thought—bringing candies to someone with stomach cancer who might at this very moment, be finding out how soon she was going to die.

I decided to walk to the University Hospital. I had written the address on a note pad in my hotel room: *24 rue Micheli-du-Crest.* But I got lost. I asked for help from passersby, most of whom spoke English, and one kind lady gave me good directions. I arrived in front of the unimposing hospital building, walked into the lobby and plopped down, exhausted, into a large leather chair. I must have waited for thirty or thirty-five minutes, until I saw Karl Gross walking down a stairway. When he saw me, he walked up and took both my hands into his.

"Well, dear Jeremy, I'm afraid I have only bad news."

"Tell me."

"Dr. Hartmann was very kind to Clara, very pleasant . . . and he made a few jokes to relax her . . . and then he took this long, thin tube with a little lens at the end—the one that I heard so much about—and he passed it through Clara's throat and into her stomach . . . and he actually saw the cancer. I know her cancer from feeling her stomach and because of her symptoms and her blood, but Hartmann actually saw it. He took a little piece of tissue for biopsy and then gave Clara something to help her rest. When Hartmann got the results, he said—"

I waited until Karl swallowed his need to cry.

"—Hartmann said 'I'm afraid there's nothing I can do for her, my dear friend. I'm sorry.'"

"Does Clara know?" I asked.

"Yes, she knows. She woke up half an hour ago, and when she saw me standing near her bed she sat up and said, 'No good, Karl. It's no good, is it?' I never lie to patients. Anyway, with that one what good would it do? She would just call me a liar. So I said, 'Yes, but I have hopes, Clara. I always have hopes.'"

"Am I allowed to see her?" I asked.

"Wait a little while. If I know her, she's probably trying to make herself look pretty again, for you. Just a little while. Room 525. I'll come back."

"Where are you going?"

"I'm going to take a nap. I'm not so young, with all this traveling and all this news, and I want to be fresh for Clara. So I'll see you, maybe in an hour."

We shook hands and he left. I saw that there was a taxi waiting to take him back to the hotel.

TWENTY-FIVE

AFTER TWENTY MINUTES I WALKED UP THE STAIRS to Room 525. I sat in one of the two straight chairs in Clara's room, watching her breathe as she slept. Karl was right—she must have gotten up earlier, because there was a blush of rouge on her cheeks and a touch of lipstick. When she sensed that someone was in the room, she sat bolt upright.

"Jeremy?"

I got up quickly and took her hand. She was very hoarse, creaking and croaking from high notes to low, as she tried to talk.

"I'm right here, Clara."

"How do you like my voice?" she squeaked, still a little groggy from the anesthesia.

"It's wonderfully sexy. Sounds like a creaky hinge

that needs oiling. Are you ready for a glass of Gutedel—nice and cold?"

"Ready!" she squeaked again. "Maybe even two."

"Oh my . . . Who knows what that might lead to?"

"I hope it does lead to that," she said in a desperate whisper. "I hope you'll try. I hope I don't frighten you now. I hope you still care for me. I hope I don't die before we make love again."

"Do you want to try it right now?" I asked, trying to make my joke sound as serious as I could manage.

"Let's wait a day or two," she said. "I don't want to rush you. I know you must be very tired." She giggled at her own joke and then coughed.

"Lie down, Clara. I'll hold your hand, but lie down and rest."

She lay back down.

"I'll do most of the talking," I said. "You just nod your head yes and no."

And I talked for about forty-five minutes, until a quarter to eight, asking silly questions to which she could just nod her head.

"Remember the Schwarzwalderschinkensomethin-gorother? Wasn't that delicious? Shall we meet for dinner in a few nights and try the chunks of pork with vinegar sauce? Yes? And the Schaufele, somethingor-other, served with herbed sauerkraut? Maurice says it's delicious. Shall we try it?"

Karl Gross walked in, slightly out of breath.

"I'm so sorry. I overslept my little nap. Did I hear the two of you talk about food again?" he asked as he took Clara's hand.

"She's doing all the talking, Karl. I just ask questions."

Clara kissed Karl's hand and whispered, "When can we go home?"

"Well, my dear, Dr. Hartmann says we can take you back the day after tomorrow, if you feel well enough. Would you like that, Clara?"

"Yes, I would. I have some important things to do," she squeaked as she smiled at me.

A little gong went off in the hallway and a nurse poked her head in the door. "Five minutes, please. Five minutes." She said it in French and then repeated it in English.

Clara looked heartbreakingly sad at the thought of our going. I leaned over and whispered in her ear, "Don't go away. I'll be right back."

I picked up my cloth bag full of underwear, socks,

and sundries and walked out of the room with Karl. I waited until a nurse passed us in the hallway and then I called out loudly, toward Clara's open door.

"Good night, dear! See you tomorrow!"

I led Karl across the hallway to the stairs.

"Go back to the hotel, Karl," I said very softly. "I'm going to stay a little longer."

"But the nurse and the orderlies will certainly—"

I quickly embraced him as I whispered, "I'm hoping they won't see me."

When I saw that there wasn't a nurse in sight, I whispered, "Go now, Karl. Quick!"

He gave me one of his devilish smiles and went down the stairs as I hurried back across the hall and into Clara's room.

Clara's face lit up when she saw that I really did come back. I made a "Shh" signal with my hand, crossed to the other side of her bed, took off my shoes and trousers and jacket, stuffed them into my cloth bag, and put it under the bed. Then I got into bed with Clara.

She didn't know what was happening, but she held back a giggle during this escapade. I got under the covers and squiggled down a foot or more until my head was out of sight. Then I moved close to Clara's side, hoping it would look, to a nurse, as if the bulge under the covers was all Clara.

"Don't talk," I whispered.

A nurse came in about two minutes later and said something in French. She probably, asked Clara if she needed more water or tea or something.

"Non, merci," Clara whispered, and turned over toward me, as if she were ready to go to sleep.

"She's gone," Clara whispered.

I wiggled up until my head was out of the cover.

"You're a very daring man," she whispered.

"Not always. Just when there's a beautiful woman lying next to me in bed."

"Even in a hospital?"

"Oh, that's the most fun."

I leaned over and kissed her gently. "It's time for you to go to sleep, Clara, if you want to be well enough to go home in two days."

I lifted Clara's head onto the soft spot on my left shoulder. She took my right hand and kissed it, then held on to it lightly until she fell asleep.

My conscience spoke to me very disrespectfully. *"Well, Casanova, here you are, under the covers with a beautiful woman, in a hospital bed, hiding from nurses and orderlies, and only a touch away from the cute Belgie, who is sleeping on your shoulder and who just found out that she's going to die. Have you figured out yet why you're here?"*

"Of course, stupid," I answered. "I'm here to protect and give comfort . . . to the woman I'm in love with."

TWENTY-SIX

THE NEXT MORNING, CLARA WAS SLEEPING PEACE-fully as the sun lit up the window shade in her room. I didn't want to wake her, so I slipped out of bed, reached for my cloth bag, and tiptoed out of the room. I stopped at the doorway to see if there were any nurses in sight, then quietly crossed the hallway, went down the stairs, and left the hospital.

Two days later, on Thursday morning, July 12, Clara, Karl Gross, and I took the train to Freiberg, where Herr Kreiss was waiting to drive us back to Badenweiler.

The trip wasn't sad or somber—I think because Clara was happy to be going back to a place that felt as close to "home" as any she knew, and also where she had been happy. It was a sunny day, and when Clara saw the rolling lavender hills as we approached the out-skirts of Badenweiler, she squeezed my hand and said, "This is good picnic weather, isn't it?"

TWENTY-SEVEN

I THOUGHT I WAS CURED OF MY CRAZINESS. AFTER we returned to Badenweiler and got settled into the Sommer Hotel again, Clara took a little nap before dinner and I went for a quiet stroll through the village. I needed to breathe some fresh air.

I walked into the bakery, the butcher shop, the cheese shop—just to smell things that were different from the smells in a hospital.

I went into a children's clothing store. It seemed that they specialized in baby clothes because there were photographs of babies on all the walls, dressed in a variety of different outfits. I saw one particular photograph that looked like a photo of me when I was three years old. My mother used to show it to me when she was going through her photo albums. She mailed that same photo to me years later, when I was on tour and she was ill and in the hospital. It had a lipstick mark on my little face, with the quote, "I kiss you, darling—now, as I did then." It was signed "Mama." She died a few days later.

The craziness didn't happen in that children's store; it happened when I walked to the edge of the village and suddenly climbed the tallest tree in sight. Don't ask me why. I climbed so high that I didn't know how I was going to get down. I must have been at least thirty feet off the ground when I saw a man walking below me, carrying a loaf of bread under his arm. I hollered as loudly as I could and I know he heard me because he looked up and waved, but then he walked away. I didn't know if he understood that I was in a panic or if he was just waving to be friendly. After five minutes, a policeman came with a fire truck. A ladder was raised and the policeman helped me down. When I was asked, in the policeman's very halting English, what the hell I was doing up in that tree, I quickly made up a story about trying to save a poor cat who looked terribly frightened. The policeman looked at me with a pained expression, then said something in German, which I roughly translated as "I think you're nuts."

* * *

AFTER I got back to the spa, I showered and shaved, put on a fresh suit and shirt—wearing my new Geneva tie that I thought Clara would like—and walked to the Garden café. Clara was later than usual and I started to worry until I saw her walk in. She waved to me as I got up, but as she came closer, I saw that her face was moist and white.

"You didn't have to rush, Clara. I would have waited for you." I helped her into her usual chair.

"I'm fine. I don't want you worrying about me, Jeremy," she said. "I'm not a cripple, you know."

I leaned over and felt her forehead.

"You have a fever, Clara. I'm taking you back to your room."

"Oh no . . . oh no, please. I wanted this evening to be so pleasant."

"It will be—once I get you back to your bed and call Dr. Gross."

As she started to get up, she said, "I'm sorry. Please forgive me."

"Stop talking nonsense and let me help you. Just take my arm and lean on me."

"Everyone will think I'm drunk."

"Good! That's what we want. Shall we sing a little song and act tipsy?"

"No, no. Don't do that. I know that you would, but don't," she said, half in panic and half in a giggle.

TWENTY-EIGHT

AN HOUR LATER, CLARA WAS LYING IN BED IN A light blue nightgown while Karl Gross examined her, listening to her heart, taking her temperature—which was 101 degrees Fahrenheit—pressing on her lymph nodes and tapping her chest with his fingers. He felt her ankles and wrists. I sat watching near the back of the room. I had learned a bit of this routine when my mother was ill. When Karl was finished, he patted Clara's hand.

"Well, my dear, I think you did a little too much for a young woman who just left the hospital and takes a train ride and takes a car ride and wants to jump right back into life and start climbing mountains the moment she arrives home. . . . Yes? Nothing serious," Karl said, looking straight at me when he said it, "but you must get lots of rest, eat healthy food . . . and save your mountain climbing for a little while," he added, looking at me again with that lovely twinkle in his eyes. "Do you think you can manage that?"

Before she could answer, I rose and said, "Yes, she can."

"Good! Look what a luxury you have, Clara. Two wonderful doctors to take care of just one patient. You are a lucky woman."

She smiled politely, quite aware that Dr. Gross was coating everything with his optimistic cheeriness.

"Now I have ordered a big pot of soup for you, with plenty for Jeremy, also. It has good broth and vegetables and basil and a little garlic, and I want you to drink as much as you can. I'm sure that Dr. Webb will see to that, won't you, Doctor?"

"I promise," I answered.

"And if you're very good, Clara, tomorrow you can have a little wine, also. But just a little. So good night, my dear child."

He gave Clara a kiss on the forehead.

"Jeremy," he said to me, "you know how to take a temperature?"

"Yes, I do."

"Good. I left the thermometer on the desk, in the little glass with alcohol in it. Let me know if her temperature goes up or down, please."

"Yes, sir."

"Good night, my boy," he said, squeezing my hand extra tightly. "I'm just across the road if you need me," he said, as he left the room.

When Karl was gone, I rubbed my hands together.

"Well now . . . What shall we do till the soup comes? Cards? Checkers? Chess? Sex? Gin rummy? Pinochle?"

"WAIT!" she cried out. "What did— What was— Did you just say sex?"

"SEX?" I said. "Are you crazy? At a time like this? You shouldn't have such thoughts on your mind right now. You're in bed with a temperature. It's much too early to be thinking about naughty things like that. We need to wait at least another day."

She looked at me with that Svengali glare of hers. "I know what you did," she said. Then she started to laugh. "All right. I can wait a day or two. Then will you stick to your word?"

There was a knock, knock on the door.

"Depends on how much soup you drink," I said as I went over to open the door.

A waiter wheeled in a covered tureen of steaming hot soup that rested on a rolling cart. I thanked the waiter and after he left I wheeled the cart over to Clara's bed. When the sides were down the cart became a small table. There were two soup bowls, two spoons, two knives, four soft rolls, a plate of butter, and two large napkins. A big ladle was resting beside the tureen.

"Do you want to have your soup in bed, Clara? Maybe you should . . . or would you be more comfortable sitting down at this little table?"

"I'll sit with you at the table. We can pretend we're in the Garden café again. Would you pour our soup? I just want to go to the bathroom for a minute."

I filled each bowl with soup and vegetables, split two rolls and buttered each half, and pulled two chairs up to our table. Karl must have told the kitchen to give us enough soup for six people.

When Clara came out of the bathroom I helped her into her chair.

"First, let me take your temperature before you eat," I said. "The soup is hot and I don't want your temperature to shoot up because of the soup."

"You really are a doctor," she said.

I took the thermometer, shook it down, placed it under her tongue, and waited for sixty seconds, staring at how pretty Clara looked, fever and all. When I took the thermometer out it was still 101 degrees.

"The same. That's all right—soup and a little kissing and a good night's sleep—that should do the trick."

Clara ate one and a half bowls of soup. They were small bowls, but she was trying her best. She also ate half of a buttered roll. It was a good start.

At nine-thirty I helped her back into bed although she didn't really need help, but it was nice to embrace her again.

"I suppose you want me to kiss you?" I asked.

"You are a naughty boy. Well, yes, I do."

"Well, ask me!" I said.

"Would you like to kiss me?" she said, with a crooked smile.

"Yes, I would," I said.

I leaned over and kissed her tenderly for at least a minute.

"Now time for sleep," I said. "Dream of pleasant

things . . . dream of two fawns watching us as we lay on the blanket in the woods, hugging each other."

Clara held my hand for a few seconds, holding back a reservoir of sadness as she stared at me. Then she smiled and said: "Good night, dearest."

TWENTY-NINE

THE NEXT MORNING I HAD SOME TEA AND THEN rushed over to Clara's room, but the receptionist said that she had been taken to the local hospital in Baden-weiler. He told me where it was located, which was actually almost next door to the tree I climbed to save the cat that wasn't there. I ran, then walked for a few seconds to catch my breath, and then ran again. In ten minutes I was there.

When I arrived in Clara's room, Karl Gross was standing over her, checking all the tubes that were coming out of her thin face and body. I stood in the back of the room, near the entrance, and whispered, "What happened, Karl?"

"Her temperature went to one hundred and four last night, Jeremy. Since we went to Geneva she doesn't eat much or drink enough water, so I decided to hydrate her."

"May I come closer, so she can see me?"

"Yes, yes. Stand at the foot of the bed so she won't have to move her head too much."

I walked to the foot of the bed until she could see me.

"Look who's here, Clara!" Karl said cheerfully. "Of all people, who do you think came to see you?"

Despite her tubes, which made her look like a mechanical doll, she broke into a big smile. Her tiny bare feet were sticking out of the blanket.

"Would you like to kiss me now?" she asked, with her sarcastic grin.

"Yes, I would," I said. I leaned down and kissed her left foot. "Oh my," I said, fondling her little toes, "I forgot what a good kisser you are."

She started to laugh so hard that Dr. Gross had to warn both of us to calm down and behave. I came closer and held her hand.

"Well, shall we get out of here and go on a picnic, Clara?"

She looked at Dr. Gross, who seemed to enjoy our banter. I knew he was happy to see her smile again.

"Oh, I would wait for at least an hour, just to be safe," Karl said, as he joined our little game.

"Well, what shall we do while we're waiting, Clara?" I asked. "Do you want to play checkers or chess or sex or gin rummy or pinochle again?"

"Would you like to marry me?" she asked.

Both Karl and I were startled, but we both assumed she was carrying on with our silly game.

"Yes, I would," I answered.

"Well, ask me!" she said.

I looked at her eyes and realized that she was serious, which, to my surprise, didn't panic me in the slightest. I took her hand.

"Would you marry me, Clara?" I asked.

"Yes, I would."

As I stared at her blue eyes, it was difficult to decide if she was saying these things because she felt so close to death and wanted to hear the words before she died . . . or if it had nothing to do with death, but rather something that she had on her heart and had the courage to say out loud.

I turned to Karl, who, by the expression on his face, was torn between medicine and love. "Can you help us, Karl?" I asked.

He paused while he tried to weigh all of these silly but probably momentous things.

"You know . . . the mayor of Badenweiler can marry you. Would you like me to ask him to come here?"

He looked at Clara first, then at me.

"Yes, please. Ask him to come," I said, looking at Clara, who beamed.

THIRTY

THE MAYOR, OSKAR KLEIN, WAS A GENTLE MAN IN his mid-fifties with soft, round features and curly grey and white hair. He was humorous, serious, intelligent, and always very gentle.

Maurice, the waiter, and Karl Gross were our two resident witnesses. I had asked Maurice to please find Mr. Chekhov and tell him that I would be honored if he came to the local hospital, very quickly, to attend the wedding of Mrs. Mulpas and Mr. Webb. When Chekhov arrived he was slightly out of breath, but he had a sweeter smile on his face than any I had seen before. He stood at the back of the room, making sure that Clara couldn't breathe any of the air that he exhaled.

Clara, with all the tubes removed, sat in a chair. I stood beside her as Karl introduced us to the mayor.

"Oskar, this is our dear Clara Mulpas . . . and this is our dear friend, Mr. Jeremy Spencer Webb."

The mayor began the service in a casual way—in English, for my sake I assumed—saying what a pleasure it was for him to meet such nice people and that he hoped to see us again if we should come back to Badenweiler, after our honeymoon. I didn't look at Clara when he said that. I just nodded a thank-you to him.

"My friends," the mayor continued, without referring to any book or bible, "I have just a few words on this happy occasion." (I'm sure Doctor Gross had instructed him carefully.) "My only advice," Mayor Klein continued, "as someone who has been married forty years now, is just to be kind to each other and hold on to this love that you have. It is more precious than any other treasure you might find."

No preaching, just a heartfelt sentiment. Good! I was grateful to him for that.

"Clara Mulpas, do you want to marry this man, and love him and stay with him for as long as you shall live?"

"Yes, I do."

"Jeremy"—he had to look at a little card he held in his hand—"Jeremy Spencer Webb, do you want to marry this dear lady, and love her and stay with her for as long as you shall live?"

"Yes, I do."

"Then, by the authority I have been granted, I pronounce you . . . husband and wife."

I was overwhelmed when I heard those words—much more than this womanizing, confirmed bachelor ever thought he would be. I leaned down, dripping a tear onto Clara's pale face, and kissed my wife.

THIRTY-ONE

AFTER FIVE DAYS, CLARA WAS RELEASED FROM THE hospital. Her temperature had been normal for three days and Karl thought it would do her good to get out of the medical atmosphere and have some time with her husband.

He also suggested that Clara not move out of her room at the Sommer Hotel; he wanted to be able to see her at all times, just in case she had any physical troubles which, he told me privately, I should expect.

On Clara's first night out we went to the Garden café, naturally. Maurice looked over us like a mother hen guarding her chicks. Clara had the soup with vegetables, basil, and garlic, which she loved so much, and I had figs and Parma ham. We shared a *poussin*. "Sharing," to Clara, meant that I ate four fifths and she had two small bites. But she liked the scalloped potatoes that came with the chicken and she ate quite a bit of them, for which I was very proud of my wife. "Proud of my wife"—a phrase I never thought I would say, or even think.

"Now listen, my little cherub," I said, "I know you're a tough lady, but I think we should put off more strenuous and emotional . . . and loving activities . . . for at least another day or two, if you agree."

"I agree—but just for a day or two."

THIRTY-TWO

Two days later, I rented the resort's plough horse from a man named Herr Bonhoffer, who owned the horse, and who was responsible for all of the garden vegetables that were grown in the two-acre field just south of the spa. "Charger," as the horse was called, ploughed the field in the early spring to get the ground ready for planting. But now, in July, the horse was just taking a lazy vacation.

Herr Bonhoffer's price for renting Charger was to be paid in German marks only, not in francs. I supposed that this was because he was an elderly German man who didn't understand anything that was French. But five marks for five hours for Charger was certainly a reasonable price.

It was a beautiful, sunny day and normally I wouldn't have worried about jackets or sweaters, but I told Clara to please bring a sweater in case the weather were to suddenly change. No colds for my wife.

I lifted Clara onto Charger's back. The horse wasn't wearing a saddle—first, because Clara said she was brought up riding horses, and second, because Charger didn't have a saddle.

I gave Clara our blanket to hold. It had cushions wrapped inside and I carried the picnic basket. I took hold of Charger's reins and off we went: "Sir Jeremy" leading "Lady Clara" and her steed, through the foothills of the Schwarzwald, always keeping an eye out for any dragons that might be in the neighborhood.

When we reached our small grassy plateau, I helped Clara down. She spread the blanket while I led Charger to the stream, so he could have a cool drink. Then I tied his reins, very loosely, around a nearby tree that was surrounded with tall grass, and I walked back to Clara.

She had our lunch laid out on the blanket: green beans, broccoli, cauliflower, carrots—I would bet this was an order from Dr. Gross to the chef—plus a dipping sauce, two large napkins, and a very small jar filled with Gutedel. I twisted off the lid and we each took a sip. The wine wasn't "nice and cold," but it was fine, and still fairly cool.

We ate our vegetables like good children, just as Karl must have envisioned. When Clara had eaten enough, she lay back onto one of the cushions and gave me one of her unmistakable looks, half smile and half invitation. I lay down next to her and she snuggled into my arms.

"Would you like to be inside me?" she asked.

As always, direct and to the point. If only I could learn that virtue from her one day. I wonder, *How many days with her do I have left?*

"Yes, I would," I answered.

She sat up, took off her sweater and started unbuttoning her pink and lavender blouse.

"Would you help me off with this long skirt? . . . I'm too excited to deal with it."

I helped her off with her skirt and her long slip and then I got undressed. Clara slipped off her pink underpants. When we were both naked, I lay down beside her and started to kiss her, when she suddenly popped her head up.

"Is my breath all right? There was some garlic in—"

"Your breath is fine. Very tasty."

I kissed her as I touched her, and she held on to what she called my willy.

"This is fun," she said. "Are you ready, dear?"

"Yes."

When I entered her, she didn't jump or get as emotional as she did the only other time we made love. She was relaxed, and when she looked into my eyes as she reached her climax, she smiled and half-whispered, "Thank you, darling."

Shortly after we made love, I pulled Clara's sweater over her shoulders so she wouldn't be cold. After she put on her underpants we sat on the blanket, sipping a little more wine.

"Gustav never wanted me to touch his willy."

"What an ignoramus," I said.

"He kissed me on my lips once in a while, but he never wanted to touch my body, or any of my intimate places—just wanted to pump away until he reached his climax. Then he'd get up quickly and smoke a cigar.

She was deep in thought for almost a minute and then asked me something that took me completely by surprise.

"Would you teach me to play a musical instrument, Jeremy? I don't mean the piano."

"Oh! Well, let me see. How about . . . What if I taught you to play a concertina? It's not too difficult and it wouldn't take up all of your precious breath."

"A concertina?"

"Yes, it's like a small accordion that you just squeeze in and out, and it has little keys on each side that you press to get the melody. What do you think?"

She looked thrilled.

"That's perfect. Thank you, dear."

"Yes, but I want something in return," I said.

"Oh? Do you mean right now?" she said with a tiny grin.

"No, no, it doesn't have to be right now, although we could start now and continue later."

"Are you sure?" she asked, completely puzzled.

"Yes, I'm sure."

"What are we talking about?" she asked.

"I want you to give me French lessons."

"Honestly?"

"Yes. Don't look so surprised. If my wife speaks French, I want to be able to speak French. Concertina for French lessons—is that a deal?"

She hugged me and said, *"Je t'aime."*

"What does that mean," I asked.

"You'll have to wait for your first French lesson to find out."

We started to pack up our lunch things. As I was reaching for my trousers, Clara said, "Why don't we wade into the stream—just up to our bellies? Then I'll feel nice and clean before putting on that silly skirt again."

I walked over to the stream and put my feet into the water while Clara and Charger watched me. The water had warmed from the sun. Cool but not cold.

"All right, but just up to your belly."

We both took off our underwear again and waded into the stream. Clara washed herself and afterward I wiped Clara's legs dry with the cloth napkins that we hadn't even used. I helped her on with her slip and skirt, pulled off her sweater so she could put on her blouse, and then slipped her sweater back on.

When we were dressed, I boosted Clara onto Charger and led them both through the hidden dangers in the enchanted forest, back to the castle in Badenweiler.

THIRTY-THREE

THE NEXT FOUR WEEKS WERE BEAUTIFUL, BUT
Clara asked if we couldn't be together when she went to
sleep, because she would often wake up in the middle
of the night and get terribly frightened. Even though
Karl Gross had suggested that Clara not move out of
her room, so that he could see her at all hours in case of
an emergency, I requested a one bedroom suite in our
hotel and told Karl that if Clara showed even the small-
est change, physically or emotionally, I would call him
and he could come right over, whatever time it was.

The suite was very comfortable, with a living room
that looked out onto the hills, a pretty bedroom with
fireplace, a large bathroom, and a small kitchenette.
The chambermaids made up what they called an "Italian double" in our bedroom, which meant tying a

large sheet around the two twin beds, making it into a double.

I sent a cable to my agent in New York:

Josh . . . I got married. I'm very happy.
Feeling fine now. Going on extended
vacation. I'll keep in touch.

Love, Jeremy.

Clara, Charger and I went on a few more picnics, but then the weather changed. There was almost a full week of rain, so we stayed at "home" and had warm meals brought to us, which consisted mostly of soup, fish, salads, and—of course—a little Gutedel in the evenings.

During the days, I gave Clara concertina lessons and she gave me French lessons. After two weeks she learned to play one of the easier Chopin preludes, which delighted her. At night, as we heard the rain pouring down while we were lying warm and cozy in our "Italian double," I finally learned what *"Je t'aime"* meant. Not so long ago I only knew what fucking meant.

THIRTY-FOUR

IN THE MIDDLE OF AUGUST SOMETHING WAS
wrong with Clara. She looked all right, but she was in
pain, terribly constipated, and she said that her whole
body ached. Fearing the worst, I called Dr. Gross. He
told me to bring her to his office immediately because
he wanted all of his equipment nearby and wanted to
take some blood, which he had been doing on a weekly
basis.

Karl examined Clara slowly and carefully, but he
kept shaking his head from side to side. When the results of her blood came back from pathology, he just
stared at the two of us. All my fears for Clara, which I
had forced to the back of my mind, suddenly came
crashing into my heart.

"My dear child," Karl said as he looked at Clara, "you are pregnant."

I was dumbfounded. Clara took a moment to recover from the shock.

"But Karl, the doctor in Brussels said that I could never have children. Never!"

"Perhaps he wasn't a very good doctor. Who sent you to him?"

"Gustav, my ex-husband."

"Who was paying for the doctor?"

"Gustav."

"Don't go to that doctor again," Karl said, holding back the anger he felt at Gustav and his inept doctor friend.

"Now both of you—I don't know if this wonderful news is really wonderful—not until we find out what's happening to the cancer in Clara's stomach. I don't want it to affect the little embryo that she's carrying, but—patience! We all have to have patience right now."

Clara squeezed my hand.

"Meanwhile, I'm also happy to tell you that you've gained some weight, Clara. I expected you to lose a few pounds each week and instead you gained a few. So, thank you for eating the way I told you. But, much more important, you've been in love, which is not only good for the appetite, but very good for having babies. Now please, both of you, go and relax, which of course is impossible. I want to call Geneva."

THREE DAYS later, Karl received a "gastro scope" from Dr. Hartmann. Karl had watched Hartmann perform the fairly simple procedure and he was feeling confident. Clara was lightly sedated and I was allowed to stay in the room.

Karl placed the tube into Clara's mouth and gently guided it down, into her stomach, and there he finally saw what he was looking for . . . Nothing! He let out a very quiet burst of joy and continued looking for a while longer, but the cancer was gone.

TWO HOURS later, Clara and I sat in Karl's office, sipping herbal tea as he spoke to us.

"I've heard of this kind of remission and read about it, and I've just talked to Dr. Hartmann about it, but I've never seen it. He said that the few patients he knows of who have had such a remission, all had an infection first and then a high fever . . . and once in a great while, the tumor disappears."

Clara smiled through her tears while she squeezed my hand.

"As a scientist I don't believe that God decides such things," Karl said. "But the immune system—that's a different story. Like an army, it gets ready to fight the first infection, which you had in your lungs, Clara, and after it kills the infection, sometimes it gets so angry that it just keeps on marching and kills the second, much more dangerous enemy. So, you had a nice infection and a very high fever and a great army to fight battles for you—and here you are, with just terrible constipation and nausea . . . Isn't that wonderful? I told you, I always have hopes."

THIRTY-FIVE

FOR THE SAKE OF A HEALTHY BABY, KARL ADVISED us to wait until October before taking the trip to New York, where I owned a small but unique home that once, before automobiles took over for horses, was a carriage house. We decided to name our baby Emily, if it was a girl, and Spencer, if it was a boy.

On October 15th we said our good-byes. Clara went to Karl's office. I told her that I'd join her in a few minutes; I wanted to see Chekhov one more time. I was told he was in the Garden café, eating whatever he was told to eat these days.

His face lit up when he saw me, but he looked paler than usual.

"How nice to see you, Jeremy. I was hoping you'd drop by."

"We're leaving today, Anton."

"So I've heard. Crossing the ocean on a big ship should be wonderful this time of year, if the weather holds."

"May I shake your hand, Anton?"

"No. I'm sorry. We've got to protect that baby, you know. Tell me something, will you?"

"Of course."

"Have you had any more of your amusing attacks lately?"

"You mean, when I go a little crazy?"

"Yes."

"Well, if you call climbing a tree in Badenweiler to save a cat that wasn't there, and then having to be rescued by a fire truck, 'amusing,' then yes. Just that once. But at least I was alone this time."

"Just you and the cat, eh?"

"Just the two of us."

"Well, that shows improvement," he said with a twinkle in his eyes. "And Karl says that Clara is feeling well, yes?"

"Yes, she is."

"Good luck, Jeremy. Write me a letter once in a while, will you? I told you—I don't like to be alone."

"I will."

"And, if you don't mind, I'd like to know how it goes when you start giving concerts again."

"Good-bye, Anton."

I WALKED into Karl's office just in time to catch a few falling tears. He gave both of us a warm hug. I could see that it was difficult for him to let go of Clara.

"I'll take good care of her, Karl. I promise."

"I know you will. I know you will. It's just—hard to say good-bye to some people."

Karl walked us out to the car, where Herr Kreiss was waiting. Karl kissed Clara one more time and then we got in. As the car pulled away, Clara turned down the window to wave. Karl hollered after us:

"Send me pictures of my godchild."

THIRTY-SIX

S.S. BREMEN

OCTOBER 19, 1903

Dear Anton,
The voyage is beautiful and Clara is eating well,
enjoying the lovely ocean air. Each afternoon we
sit on deck, in lounge chairs, and have our tea
and scones. Clara has herbal tea and I have my
Earl Grey, of course. The steward covers us both
with soft, warm blankets.

   You were right, of course. I wasn't "exploding
with anger" at that music critic who said I didn't
show any true emotion when I played my violin. I
went crazy in the middle of my concert in Cleve-
land when I realized that he was right.

I hope you're not too lonely. I'll write again soon.

> *With warm regards,*
> *Jeremy*

P.S. By the way, that infamous music critic from New York has very dark hair . . . almost as black as the sharps and flats on a Steinway piano.

THIRTY-SEVEN

WE LANDED AT THE PORT OF NEW YORK ON OCTO-
ber 27. My little carriage house is nestled between two
other homes on a quiet street called Minetta Lane. The
house is a duplex and has a small guest bedroom, just
right for the baby. As I had hoped, Clara loves the
house.

I practice on my violin three to four hours a day, this
gives Clara a chance to get to know the shops in our
neighborhood. She also began knitting.

I visited my agent and told him that we were back
and happy, and I wanted to work again, but that I
would need more practice time before playing with an
orchestra. I also said that I only wanted engagements
that were close to New York. "I'm going to be a father,
you see."

I don't believe in miracles—unless, of course, they happen to me. In Clara's fourth month she held my hand against her abdomen and I felt a little kick from "our" fetus. I couldn't tell if it was a girl kick or a boy kick.

On April 3, Emily Webb was born: seven pounds, three ounces.

On April 27, I played Beethoven's Violin Concerto with the New York Philharmonic. The next day I got the following review from that same infamous music critic:

> Last night, violinist Jeremy Spencer Webb performed Beethoven's Violin Concerto in D Major. As always, he was an exquisite technician, but last night true emotion poured from his heart and through his violin.

I sent the review to Anton.

On July 15, 1904, Anton Chekhov died in Baden-weiler, Germany. By mistake, his body was sent to Moscow in a refrigerated railway car that had a painted sign on the outside that read FRESH OYSTERS. If Anton knew, I think he would have laughed out loud . . . and then wished he had written it into one of his short stories.

Enjoy Gene Wilder's fiction debut along with his acclaimed autobiography

"Gene Wilder's delightful fiction debut—a novel so witty, dramatic, and romantic that the reader is left with an indelible mental movie."
—*Los Angeles Times*

"Pure Gene Wilder! Uproariously funny and at times very moving. It made me want to go out and see every Gene Wilder movie again."
—Mel Brooks